"I Want Th...
Past The Six-Month Arrangement..."

The very air seemed to still Matt's words. Perri froze, staring hard into his eyes.

"I don't have much to give you. But I want a chance," Matt continued. "Can you forgive me for the past?"

"Yes, I can forgive you, Matt," Perri said simply and without hesitation. "You're the father of my child. And I love you. And most importantly, I want the past behind us so I don't have it hanging over me and this baby."

Cradling her in his arms, Matt buried his face in her throat. "Then we'll call it done," he said, moved by her declaration of love.

"Matt," she asked, "why did you move my things into your room?" She could feel his body go tense.

"Because you're the mother of my child. And because"— he paused, looking straight into her eyes "—you're where you've always belonged, Perri," Matt continued. "And where I need you to be...."

Dear Reader,

Spring is in the air—and all thoughts turn toward love. With six provocative romances from Silhouette Desire, you too can enjoy a season of new beginnings…and happy endings!

Our March MAN OF THE MONTH is Lass Small's *The Best Husband in Texas.* This sexy rancher is determined to win over the beautiful widow he's loved for years! Next, Joan Elliott Pickart returns with a wonderful love story— *Just My Joe.* Watch sparks fly between handsome, wealthy Joe Dillon and the woman he loves.

Don't miss Beverly Barton's new miniseries, 3 BABIES FOR 3 BROTHERS, which begins with *His Secret Child.* The town golden boy is reunited with a former flame—and their child. Popular Anne Marie Winston offers the third title in her BUTLER COUNTY BRIDES series, as a sexy heroine forms a partnership with her lost love in *The Bride Means Business.* Then an expectant mom matches wits with a brooding rancher in Carol Grace's *Expecting….* And Virginia Dove debuts explosively with *The Bridal Promise,* when star-crossed lovers marry for convenience.

This spring, please write and tell us why you read Silhouette Desire books. As part of our 20th anniversary celebration in the year 2000, we'd like to publish some of this fan mail in the books—so drop us a line, tell us how long you've been reading Desire books and what you love about the series. And enjoy our March titles!

Regards,

Joan Marlow Golan
Senior Editor, Silhouette Desire

Please address questions and book requests to:
Silhouette Reader Service
U.S.: 3010 Walden Ave., P.O. Box 1325, Buffalo, NY 14269
Canadian: P.O. Box 609, Fort Erie, Ont. L2A 5X3

THE BRIDAL PROMISE
VIRGINIA DOVE

SILHOUETTE *Desire*

Published by Silhouette Books

America's Publisher of Contemporary Romance

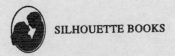

SILHOUETTE BOOKS

ISBN 0-373-76206-2

THE BRIDAL PROMISE

VIRGINIA DOVE

grew up in a small town in Oklahoma, where Route 66 and the Chisholm Trail intersect. After graduating from Southern Methodist University, she came to New York City, where she began a successful career as a dancer under her stage name and performed on Broadway in such musicals as *My Fair Lady, Best Little Whorehouse In Texas* and *Chicago*. Currently she lives in New York City with her husband, and she still twirls a mean baton.

Many thanks to Melissa Senate.
And as always, all my love to Lexie.

Prologue

Seventeen-year-old Perri Stone stood before a louvered window at Gledhill and carefully opened the gold locket that hung around her neck. The diamond hidden inside the oval sparkled as it caught the light of the setting sun. She tilted the locket back and forth, mesmerized by the way the rays bounced off the faceted stone.

Soon, she would be able to put Matt's picture inside. Soon, it would be all right for everyone to know they were getting married. Soon, they wouldn't have to sneak around and hide the truth. Just as soon as Matt explained things to his parents, everything would be all right.

Perri closed the locket on a kiss and whirled around Gannie Gledhill's formal living room. Gannie was the closest thing to a grandmother Perri had in Spirit Valley, Oklahoma. She had taken a special interest in Perri and in Matt, long before they had ever fallen in love. Even as children, Matt and Perri had never doubted that Gannie loved them both as if they were her own.

Dancing over to the fireplace, Perri studied each object on the mantel and reasoned out how to proceed. Maybe this evening they would tell Gannie of their plans. It wouldn't be any surprise to her. Gannie knew that they were very much in love. They had been meeting here at Gledhill for nearly a year.

Soon, she thought, I'll be eighteen and everything will be all right. Her fingers closed over an arrowhead that had lived on the mantel ever since Matt had found it out by the horse barn. Its edges were still razor sharp; but the meticulous, hand-chipped surface had been worn smooth by time. She gripped the stone hard enough to hurt. Please, she prayed, let the old scandal and the bad blood between our families no longer matter.

Perri closed her eyes and tried to imagine how her mother was going to react to the news. Janie Stone had her own reasons for wanting her girl to stay away from the Ransoms. But Gannie would bring her around. Perri was sure of it. Perri Ransom. She considered how it sounded for maybe the millionth time. Mrs. Matthew Ransom.

The sound of a car pulling up the drive drew her back to the window, expecting to see Gannie on her way to the garage. Instead, Perri's blood froze as Leila Ransom, Matt's mother, got out of her car. For a time, Mrs. Ransom simply studied the old Gledhill farmhouse. Then she stalked onto the porch and through the front door. Leila Ransom moved into the living room like a predator closing in for a quick, clean kill.

"Are you pregnant?" Leila asked calmly, her lovely green eyes resembling ice crystals.

Speechless, Perri shook her head.

"If you find out that you are, I'll pay for an abortion. You'll need one because Matt isn't going to marry you, no matter what he's told you. He has more pride than that and more concern for his position in this community." Leila glanced at the clock on the mantel. Her expression suggested she might find it amusing to time their exchange. "He's done with you, dear," she said, "believe me."

Perri couldn't hide her sense of shock or her helpless anger. Never had she imagined herself in a showdown with Matt's mother. She was in over her head and she knew it.

"I do hope you will listen to me," Leila cautioned, "because I don't plan to give you a second chance. If you continue to see

my son, I'll make certain you regret it." Pale blond curls re-
bounded as Leila turned toward the front windows.

"Certain well-placed rumors, about how your precious little
mother has been having an affair with my husband for years,
won't be too difficult to arrange. Everyone will know that's the
real reason behind her divorce. And everyone in town will believe it. Don't think they won't." Amused now, she nailed Perri
with those inhuman eyes.

"Never doubt that I can do it or that I will, Perri. The fact
that it's a lie will mean nothing when I've finished with her. I'd
enjoy the opportunity," Leila added as an afterthought. "That
goody-goody act of hers won't be of much help by the time I'm
done.

"No," Leila smiled coldly, "I think it would be best for you
to take your daddy up on the chance to go to that special high
school, the one I heard your mother bragging about. Leave for
Raleigh and spend your senior year living with your father and
his new family. And stay away from my son." Leila thoughtfully
adjusted her wristwatch, pausing to tap a perfectly manicured nail
against the crystal.

The sound struck Perri as inordinately loud, empty and hollow.
She flinched away as if from a blow.

"Maybe they've got some summer courses. Now that's an
idea," Leila brightened. "You could leave immediately after
school is out.

"And," she shrugged delicately, "if you don't, when I'm
done with her, your precious momma will have to leave town.
Do I make myself crystal clear?"

Perri began to tremble as Leila closed in for the kill. "Yes,
ma'am," she whispered. It was over. Every hope and dream had
been shattered.

"Never mention any of this conversation to Matt, ever," Leila
ordered. "Do we understand each other?"

"Yes, ma'am." Tight-lipped and terrified, Perri didn't even
realize she was in shock. All she knew was an overwhelming
sense of hopelessness and loss.

"Good." Leila sighed with satisfaction, glancing at the mantelpiece. She walked out and drove away without another word.

Unable to move, Perri found herself staring blindly at the ticking clock. Cruelty had worked wonders. And so quickly.

Perri never cried.

One

Twelve years later

Matt Ransom was not in the mood for a tornado. Although with his luck, it probably wouldn't be a twister. It would probably be something he couldn't out-dodge, like more baseball-sized hail.

It was hard to complain about tornadoes in Tornado Alley without feeling just a little silly; but he had a mind to anyway. He knew his brother, Whit, was watching helplessly as almost two thousand acres blew away in the Oklahoma Panhandle. Just two inches of rain since November had left many with no choice but to sell their cattle. And there hadn't been even a hope of a wheat crop for Whit. Irrigation did little good when forty-five-to-fifty-mile-an-hour winds raged day after day.

At least around Spirit Valley, Oklahoma, there would be a harvest, of sorts. Blessed by the river and many deep wells, in addition to a man-made lake, Spirit was outside of the burn ban. Every field was full of short oats.

"By now, the wheat should be dropping its heads, dammit," he muttered as in frustration he automatically checked the land and the sky.

Understanding that others were having it worse didn't make his own situation any less aggravating. When racing against a storm, it was usually the storm that won the race. Today wasn't going to be an exception. Something was in the air and he could smell it. So far, it was only black clouds, some serious wind and approaching dense rain. Born for and of the land, Matt held no hope it would stay as it was now.

The stop signs and stoplights he now had to navigate were giving him the blues. His father still couldn't reconcile himself to the fact that the town had grown to need them. Too many people. Matt had grown up seeing those stop signs removed at the start of every harvest. The wheat-laden combines coming in from the farms had made their way into Spirit Valley without a hitch. There was a time when every kid in town knew not to cross Elm Street without being very careful during June.

Matt swore silently as he stopped at yet another light. Harvest was vital to the whole community. The combines would roll on through, from the farms to the grain elevators over by the railroad tracks, as fast as the weather would allow. "Stopping every couple of blocks is just uncivilized," he grumbled as he floated the last four lights.

At the moment, Matt had a fractious yearling that he wanted ready for the sale coming up at Shawnee. Salem didn't appreciate the hole in the roof over his stall and didn't care who knew it. *A paint with an attitude; just what I need.* Matt shook his head at his own lame joke. He had to get out of town. It was affecting his brains.

He had a dozen things to do today without having to repair the damage from yesterday's hail. "All right, I was lucky," he acknowledged as he slapped the steering wheel with the heel of one broad hand. It was only one building. At least his father's roof was undamaged.

Not that Sam Ransom would let his oldest son know if he needed any help. The two of them hadn't had a true conversation about anything other than horses or hard work since before Matt's mother, Leila, had passed away. And that had been years ago. Matt knew he was responsible for the distance between them and he accepted that. Yet of all the things that had hardened him since he'd become a man, the breach with his father still brought a daily ache. He made a mental note to check the old place himself before too many more days went by.

"Here it comes," he muttered. Big fat drops of rain began to break from the black clouds overhead.

Annoyed at the delay in repairing the roof, and fit to be tied over having to make a repair to anything this early in the season, he almost missed the fact that Gannie Gledhill's front door was open. It never occurred to him to let such a transgression slide by. As the pickup behind him honked in protest, he abruptly turned in and barreled up the drive.

Just driving toward Gledhill brought an ache to his heart. Lord, how he missed Gannie. It was too soon. He wasn't ready for her to be gone. The funeral had only been two days ago, and he couldn't seem to adjust to the loss of the only woman he'd never once doubted he could trust. But it was more than that. Gannie's death brought too many painful changes.

Gannie. Her family went back almost as far as Matt's own. Her grandfather had been sent by the Rock Island Railroad when the line had brought its rails to this part of Oklahoma. Old Man Gledhill had married a local girl, buying a farm and building a house in town. He'd had everything brought in from back East, including silk wallpaper for the dining rooms. "Got a good deal on the shipping rate," Sam Ransom used to say.

Much to her family's regret, Olivia—her given name—had refused to go back East to school. Instead she had stayed, graduated from the Oklahoma College for Women and become the town librarian. She had never married. Yet so many children over the years had found a "safe harbor" with her. Sam Ransom had given her the name of Gannie, "the town's Grannie," when he was still in grade school.

Keeper of the town's books, its heritage, and its children: to many, she was Spirit Valley. To Matt she was even more. How had he made it through the last twelve years? With Gannie's love, faith and guidance, he acknowledged. It had taken Gannie's bracing approach to keep him sane.

And staying steady and well-respected in Spirit Valley was the Ransom family's heritage. *Ransom: The price of redemption; an atonement.* Now with Gannie gone, the old house was linked in Matt's mind to only one other woman.

He could picture her laughing in the dining room; or watering the backyard. Luminous eyes had watched him as sunlight had played through the windows of an upstairs bedroom. Matt hadn't often noticed the Indian heritage in her, unless he'd looked past the light hair and eyes. But it was there. Light in that little room had branded her keen-edged cheekbones as Perri Stone had stood slim, motionless, his.

Perri's eyes, he thought. Time had frozen a memory of Perri Stone in just about every corner of that house. Perri's eyes had always intrigued him. The center of each iris was a warm, brandy-colored brown surrounded by emerald green. Matt had never considered, until now, how they were a lighter variation of his own mix of onyx and forest green. Well, that shocked him, teasing back to life some of his fury.

Driving too fast to absorb the implications of the slightly opened gate to the little graveyard and the red rose on one simple stone marker, he slammed the longbed under the carport. Matt barely felt the sudden whipping of wind and chilly rain as he took the steps of Gledhill's wraparound porch two at a time.

Whoever it was, would want to have a good reason for being on the property, because he was in no mood for any more delays. He had a full day of business to attend to, some of it sorry indeed.

Among other things, he had some horses running at Remington Park tomorrow, if the weather didn't cancel the races. And some owners had threatened to drop by in anticipation of the running. The social necessities of a well-respected horse farm were never something he could easily oblige. The screen door slammed out his frustration as his boots hit the old wooden floor.

Whoever it was had walked right on in as if he owned the place. And whoever it was, she was really in no mood for the

Spirit Valley grapevine to find out so quickly that she was moving in. Perri Stone shook loose the raindrops on her way in from garaging the car. She moved fast, hoping to head off the visitor and graciously sweep him right back out the front door.

The cowboy reached the back doorway of the living room at almost the same moment she entered. They both stuttered to a halt as recognition over small matters, like a red rose on an old grave and the identity of who *always* walked into that house like he owned it, returned to haunt her.

Jeans, boots, work shirt and cheekbones. In the low, stormy light it could have been anybody. But those cheekbones, combined with the piercing eyes and the sharp brows and nose of a hawk, meant it wasn't just anybody. Stifling the small cry wasn't an option. Her heart wished that it could be.

He uttered a low oath as she smacked into his chest, more through his refusal to give an inch than due to speed. Matt's hands reached out to hold her in a response both instantaneous and automatic. It didn't improve his mood one bit.

Perri knew to expect a storm. So far they had managed a cold, civilized distance. But until six weeks ago, when they had begun keeping vigil over Gannie's hospital bed, they hadn't shared a roof in twelve years. And the last time they had been in this room together, he'd been closer to violence than she'd ever seen him in her life.

Perri would not give him the satisfaction of seeing her go weak in the knees as he grabbed her and the sweet memories came flooding back. Her momentary relief that it was Matt in the house was rooted in the distant past, and promptly overshadowed by the reality of the present.

"Dammit, Ransom, you scared me to death!" she declared, recklessly pushing away from him.

"My pleasure, Stone," he answered coldly. Matt stared at her as he quickly let her go.

She stared right back. Then without another word, Perri moved to the television and found a weather bulletin. A tornado was passing twelve miles to the southwest of where they were stand-

ing. The open front door brought in air cold enough to tell her
to expect the sound of hail. Although she wasn't soaked from
her run back into the house, she shivered. At the moment she
had a more immediate threat to face than the approaching violence out the front door.

He moved slowly, silently behind her as she kept her eyes
glued on the weather map and tried to focus on what the weatherman had to say. It felt as if a brick wall, warmed by the sun,
had suddenly materialized at her back.

She was a tall woman. But he was a tall man, broad-
shouldered and with a long reach. Waves of heat were rolling
off of him, anger waves most likely. It couldn't be any other
kind between them. She resisted the urge to rest against him
when the meteorologist announced that Spirit Valley was out of
danger. There would be no comfort there.

Perri fought back the urge to yawn as she felt him shamelessly
look her over. Nerves had always caused her to yawn, and yawn
big, at the most inopportune moments. This time, she reasoned,
it might be more than her life was worth to succumb to the
response. She started as the erratic beat of an arriving hailstorm
further destroyed her peace of mind.

Matt eyed her critically. "You seem taller. Did you grow or
something?"

"An inch, when I turned nineteen." Perri's eyes never left the
screen.

"That must be it, then. Something seems off." He circled to
her side. "Something more personal than the fact that you're all
grown up now," he continued. "I've been meaning to tell you.
You filled out in all the right places, looks like." Matt smiled
with satisfaction when she stiffened at that remark.

She turned to face him, forcing herself to look at him as if he
were someone she could easily dismiss. "What are you doing
here, Matt?" Perri asked with just the right note of polite weariness. But it was a mistake to look him in the eye.

Matt's eyes. At first one didn't notice the variance in color.
They looked almost black, his Indian heritage plainly spelled out
in bone structure, hair and eyes. A closer look revealed the pres-

ence of dark-green shards. The result yielded eyes that seemed to absorb the light. Eyes more aged than the man. Matt looked like he hadn't truly smiled from the heart in a long time.

"I saw the front door open and stopped to check," he said, as if such a thing was obvious. It was. "You didn't waste any time running back to collect what's yours, did you?" Matt paused before saying softly, "Of course, it's only a matter of time before you run somewhere else, isn't it?"

Well, there was no answer for that, under the circumstances.

"Where's the car?" he inquired. "The garage?"

She nodded.

"Did you get everything in before the rain started?"

"You needn't concern yourself." Her answer was immediate and brisk.

"Did you get everything in?" It was a demand, not a request for information.

She shook her head, no. Her eyes dropped to his hand, as she realized he had just undone the top two buttons of her jacket. Perri wouldn't give him the satisfaction of trying to slap his hand away. If she lost her temper with him, she lost. It was that simple.

"Very funny, Matt." It simply amazed her that she could sound so damn bored while her pulse was scrambling like mad at his touch.

"Just testing a theory I have about those buttons." He looked so deceptively friendly as the nail of his index finger scraped lightly down from her collarbone to the third button, revealing skin the color of honey above the top of her lace camisole.

Perri breathed in the scent of wind and sun, horses, hay and Matt: an all-too-familiar combination she had worked very hard to forget. It was, at this moment, impossible to forget anything about him, not when he touched her.

Abruptly, he moved toward the back door. She felt the same sick, hollow sensation come over her that she had felt the day she had learned he was marrying someone else.

"You can button back up, for now. I'll get the rest of your stuff." He paused in the doorway. "And you can quit glaring at me, Stone. I'm just being neighborly. After all, we have to work together. I'm looking forward to it.''

She missed him the second he walked out the door. Dear God, how was she ever going to work with this man? She rebuttoned her jacket and finally released the breath she'd been holding. Perri moved through the front door, to the comfort of the covered porch.

The hail was beginning to play out, the small pellets clattering harmlessly off the roof. The brief storm that had passed in Gannie's living room had caused far more damage than the current weather pattern.

Perri stood there staring blindly at the honeysuckle as it took a beating from the storm. She reminded herself that she was twenty-nine years old now, not seventeen and helplessly in love with a twenty-four-year-old Matt Ransom. Those two individuals no longer existed and the ones who stood on the property today had a job to do.

Surely, they were mature enough to get it done. They would work together because they had to, for something important to both of them. He was just playing with her, she reasoned, nothing more. Just testing her for a reaction. He had made it crystal clear he didn't want her.

She had seen him change overnight into a man who would enjoy toying with her if she challenged him. Standing toe-to-toe and battling it out might be satisfying; but a calm, dignified approach was the only safe road.

Perri reminded herself that life had surely hardened Matt Ransom, that he had changed in ways she didn't understand. But no matter what she had heard in the last twelve years, he couldn't have changed that much. She wouldn't believe it of him. Intuitively she knew he would never treat a lady with anything less than respect. And, after all, this was just business. Perri Stone excelled at "just business."

She shivered as chilling rain blew onto the porch. Still mentally reassuring herself, Perri moved back into the hall. The pressure had lessened enough with the storm's passing for her to shut the door before she started up the stairs.

As she reached the second floor, Matt caught up with her. She wordlessly turned toward the back bedrooms as he automatically moved with her suitcases to the front.

He halted in the doorway of "her" room; the room where he had taken her virginity, where he'd taken her heart. "I have a choice of rooms this time and I've decided I'd rather sleep in the back." She spoke quietly, head high, back straight, as she moved down the hall toward the back bedroom overlooking the pecan trees.

Matt stood immobile, just looking into the familiar bedroom. Finally he turned and followed her, his features a complete blank. "Don't blame you," he said shortly. "You've outgrown the little room." Bringing in the suitcases, he set them down as she indicated. "You have an awful lot of stuff for somebody just passing through, haven't you?" It was a challenge.

"What makes you think I'm just passing through?" If she could find a way to slow down and stop answering him like she was a repeating rifle, she might get through this. "It will take some time to honor Gannie's request, whatever the details turn out to be," Perri said. "I'm here for a year at least, or something like that, right? That is, unless you've already heard the fine points of the will and have got it all figured out."

She turned and gazed out the window overlooking the backyard. "Have you, Matt?" she asked. "What are we supposed to do?" She didn't like the way that last question softened her.

"Do you care, Perri?" he countered. "Or do you just plan on going through the motions to fulfill the terms of the will? Gannie is gone. You're free to run for good now," he added savagely. Perri's neck arched slightly as if someone had struck her between her shoulder blades.

Matt crossed to the opposite set of windows, checking the storm's progress from the east. "Whatever we do will affect the town for some time to come. That was Gannie's plan, some sort of long-term project for improvement. Not something that can be neglected after a 'respectable' period of time." He turned to face her. The air seemed highly charged around them and suddenly the back bedroom felt very crowded.

"If you think you can get away with just going through the motions before you start looking to sell out and leave, you may as well know now that I'll buy you out with pleasure," he declared. "That would suit you, wouldn't it, Per?" She felt him move up behind her. "Then you could go back to New York or move on to someplace new."

The small insult didn't escape her. Apparently Matt figured that no home could ever mean enough to her to keep her from moving on.

"I heard you didn't even have a permanent job to give up in order to come down here," he added. "You just 'consult' here and there for a bunch of different banks, right?"

The green in Perri's eyes blazed as she turned away from the window. "Let's get this much out of the way, right now, Matt," she said angrily. "I care deeply about Spirit Valley. It was my home. And Gannie was just about the most important person in my world." The tears in her throat almost caused her voice to fail. But not quite. Perri stubbornly willed herself to go on.

"I owe her more than I can ever express. So don't think you've got any right to chastise me for having left," she went on. "I don't feel I owe you any explanations for my way of life. But please, know this: I would have given anything to have stayed home."

Time seemed to stretch to the snapping point before he gave her a rueful half smile. Her heart broke as she saw she had been right. It never really reached his eyes.

"You're not the little girl you were the last time we stood in this house," he said, shoving his hands into his back pockets. "Mistakes were made. I should never have touched you. I knew that, and I take full responsibility," Matt declared. "I was robbing the cradle but I just couldn't help myself." He looked away from the woman she had become.

"However, all that doesn't change the fact that you left. You are no longer a part of this world," Matt said coldly. "There are no bright lights here. There is nothing left for you but some stone markers in the cemetery." The very idea served to make him angrier. He turned back to face her. "What is here in Spirit Valley that could possibly make you want to stay?"

The look of pure longing she couldn't completely disguise caused them both to blush. The unguarded moment increased his fury. Warily, she started to move toward the door. Then Perri stopped, turning in frustration and maybe even some fear. Like that night twelve years ago, there was nowhere to run.

"Let's just find out right now, shall we," Matt whispered as he moved across the room and reached for her. He held her jaw firmly in his hands, those long fingers biting lightly into the back of her neck. His palms burned her as they slowly moved down her shoulders to her arms, just before his fingers gently circled her wrists.

"Do you taste the same now that you're all grown up, dar-lin'?" he asked lightly. "I've been meaning to find out ever since you got back into town." In seconds he had the answer for himself as he ruthlessly pulled her to him and his mouth took hers.

Perri's shocked intake of breath opened her mouth under his and Matt took full advantage of her surprise. His tongue probed decisively as he cuffed her wrists to the small of her back with one hand.

The electrically charged air seemed to light a spark within her Perri had long assumed to have died. She tried desperately to breathe into her burning lungs. It wouldn't have mattered if she had had a moment to think about it, or even if he hadn't molded her firmly to him. She would have opened for him anyway. She hoped that realization could remain her secret, and not a part of the battering her pride was about to take.

For Perri couldn't completely stop herself from responding as his tongue suggestively moved in and out of her welcoming mouth. Matt couldn't have made his intent more clear. She couldn't have made her assent more apparent. She melted against him and tried not to moan as he played with her mouth, delicately nipping at her lower lip.

Matt was the one who abruptly ended the kiss. He picked up the conversation right where he'd left off.

"You do taste the same," he said gruffly. "I like that. So that's what we have here," he declared as he caged her face in his hands. "Heat. That's all it can be between us, Perri. Just heat." He allowed himself one more brief, hard kiss before he released her, none too carefully. She struggled to regain her composure as he nonchalantly turned back to the window to check the sky.

"That's all I have left for any woman. So, if you're as agreeable as you seem, we could have a good time before you leave." He turned back to face her, his smile more than just a little arrogant. "But don't expect love from me, hon. Certainly not for you," he added. "It's all been burned away."

Perri's embarrassment grew as he blatantly considered her before starting for the door. It was as if nothing of any importance had happened between them. "Matt," she called, frozen to the spot where he had left her.

He paused without turning around.

"I never got to tell you how sorry I was to hear about Cadie and the babies."

He walked out without a word.

Matt was down the stairs and out the front door, his pickup making a fast retreat before she even came close to getting her breath back. "Well, that went really well," she muttered. Perri sank to the bed and rapidly worked the window open. She needed air. Immediately.

So much for the calm, ladylike approach. She couldn't have made a bigger fool of herself, if she had thought it out with both hands for two weeks. Perri rested her head against the cold metal of the window screen, inhaling the mingled smells of metal, rain and wet grass. For the longest time she couldn't move. She just stared at the yard.

It was ridiculous. He'd just kissed her senseless and walked out. Perri wondered if he'd even paused long enough to shut the front door. "I'm good at strategy and logic," she muttered. "I've got tougher clients back in Manhattan to deal with on a daily basis. I'm known for never falling apart."

Perri stopped. It had come to this—she was justifying herself to a pecan tree. This from a woman who always kept it together. A woman who had never permitted herself to test the endurance of another love.

"This is getting me nowhere," she whispered. Perri had to move. She couldn't continue to sit there as daylight burned away.

Out the door of the bedroom and halfway down the stairs, she paused and looked around at the beloved old place. Gannie's windows needed cleaning. She made a mental note to take care of that first thing. The dusty windows, more than the laying of flowers by a gravestone, caused her to feel the punch of knowing the old woman was truly gone.

Her gaze drifted into the living room as she sank down onto one of the steps. Through the rungs of the staircase she could see the memory box she had made as a gift her sophomore year in high school.

Inside the memory box, the gold railroad spike needed polishing; but the silver-plated engineer's watch didn't look quite as tarnished. It gleamed softly in the stormy light, as if just waiting for its owner to descend the stairs and retrieve it, along with his favorite pipe. It was almost as if the Rock Island Line still had some muscle in the old Indian Territory. She had chosen each of Gannie's treasures for the display with great care, the year before her world had fallen apart.

A picture of Miss Vienna Whitaker and her son, Matthew Lawrence Ransom, hung on the wall by the entrance to the living room. It had been taken in front of the tiny graveyard just outside and down the rise from the front door. Perri had stopped there on her way to the house, placing a single rose on a worn, white marker that said *Stone Baby 1889*.

Devoid of trees or bushes, with a gate that still stuck at the last, the skeletal, white iron fence and small arch sheltered thirty-one graves. It had served as a final resting place only until the town had been incorporated. Now, it was part of Perri's inheritance and therefore, her responsibility.

The porch, the pictures, the miniature graveyard, the memory box: so many things that softened the heart. So many symbols of everything she had ever hoped and dreamed of maintaining. Everything she had, at one time, thought she would miraculously have a chance to treasure now was hers by right. Now that the heart had gone out of the dream.

Perri slowly dropped her forehead onto the arm covering her knees and did what she'd been too proud to do that night twelve years before. She cried her eyes out. "Oh, Gannie," she sobbed as she sat on the stairs.

Iced cucumber slices helped soothe her swollen eyes. The task of repairing her makeup served to pull her back together. Perri armored herself in one of the few business suits she had brought with her. Most everything she had to choose from made her look like she was on her way to a funeral. She didn't kid herself. She was about to go into battle. As she locked up, she noticed the sun was on its way back. It lifted her spirits to see that for now, the storm had passed. Knowing a drive would clear her head, she headed east past the grain elevators.

On impulse, she stopped into the local florist for a half-dozen roses. Perri watched the owner's daughter take great care to arrange them in leaves and baby's breath, tissue and ribbon.

Shyly, the girl eyed Perri's business suit, with its fitted waist and mandarin collar. The severe style of dress might have gone unnoticed, but for how effortlessly it displayed her sleek, trim shape. And the fact that it was black. Nobody wore black at high noon unless they were on their way to a funeral.

Or a gunfight, Perri mused. How appropriate.

"Anything else?" the florist inquired.

"Thank you, no." Perri smiled. The teenager before her was so fresh and pretty, with the dramatic looks of the Plains Indians.

"Here's your change then," the girl chirped, making the purchase. "Y'all come back."

"I already have," Perri whispered to herself, halfway to the door.

Back inside the car, Perri placed the beautifully wrapped roses on the seat and headed for the back roads. The sky had cleared to a bright, shiny blue, and it was wonderful to get off the highway. It felt right to wind through little towns, past pastures and railroad tracks, past small ponds and under the gentle arch of the windbreaks. She stopped in the middle of the road until an egret could make up its mind which way to fly.

As she drove on, a red pickup turned onto the road in front of her. A big black rottweiler riding in back seemed to smile as they drove past old Bohemian Hall. Some of her ancestors had settled right here after the Land Run of 1889.

She followed behind as the dog and his pickup led her onto Route 66. Her eyes automatically checked a field of wheat on the driver's side of the road as she made the turn. "Short oats. That's not right," Perri muttered, frowning slightly. The wheat should be solid gold and ready to drop by now. Even she knew that.

The bridge over the railroad tracks into town looked a little shabby, and somehow smaller than Perri remembered. A World War II fighter plane, permanently parked in front of the American Legion Hall, seemed to let the traveler know he had entered another time. Spirit Valley, Oklahoma, announcing right up front that its ideals were as much a part of the past as the old plane, the tracks and the weathered bridge. Perri stopped at a light and tried to make sense of it all.

Elms lining Elm Street beyond the underpass had been planted over fifty years ago and now stood tall as she drove into the cemetery. She unwrapped the roses with her window down, listening intently. The sound of the wind filled the silence. No birds sang. At one time, hundreds of scissortails had inhabited this area.

Perri got out of the car with the separated roses. As she placed single white roses on different graves throughout the section, she asked herself what would they think? What would they do differently?

She approached a marble bench and bent to touch the new marker surrounded by funeral wreaths. Perri stared hard at the stone, before reverently covering it with the last rose. What have you gotten me into, Gannie? Rage, grief and a sort of deep, deep hurt she had always associated with the loss of innocence, warred within her.

No one but Gannie had known exactly how she had felt. No one but Gannie had ever learned all of the truth about the most important event in Perri's life: when she had lost him. "Why make it so I have to work with Matt?" she pleaded softly. "You know I'll always love him. Why put me through this kind of pain?" What plan or project could be that important?

Dry-eyed and thoroughly bewildered at the part she now had been assigned to play, Perri stared at the fluttering rose for a long time. She had wanted a tribute that wasn't staked in, fighting with the wind in order to stay.

Knowing the roses would most likely be blown apart and away before she made it out of the cemetery, she got back in the car and drove on. The sight of a martin frantically tailgating a hawk kept her from dwelling upon what lay ahead. Perri didn't look back.

Perri parked in the lot adjoining the courthouse and the professional buildings. She made her appointment dead on time. The lawyer's secretary eyed her outfit and smiled in understanding. "Go on in, Ms. Stone, please."

Perri took a deep breath, knocked once and opened the door. Help me through this, Gannie, please, she prayed as she entered the room.

"Hello, John," Perri smiled at her old friend and Gannie's champion.

The room's other occupant had obviously arrived early for their appointment and now stood with his back to the door. She noted that his stance was relaxed, as if this were *his* turf, not hers. He didn't turn around upon her arrival, but instead stood staring out the window at the now-defunct railroad depot which housed the Spirit Valley Historical Museum.

Over his shoulder, Perri could clearly see the bronze plaque declaring that this spot had been the western boundary for the Run of the Unassigned Lands. At noon on April 22, 1889, the starting gun had sounded and two million acres of Indian Territory had been opened up for the Run.

By nightfall, a tent city had sprung up on the spot where they now stood. What their ancestors had seen that day, and shortly thereafter, bore no resemblance to the view through the window over which Matt Ransom now brooded.

She crossed to the upholstered chair the attorney indicated for her use. So. It would be a war of silence rather than reproach. Very well, Perri thought grimly.

John Deepwater retrieved the folders from his desk and handed one to Perri. With the dignity and grace that was so much a part of him, he turned to Ransom and said: "Shall we begin, Matt?"

Without a word, Matt took the file and his seat.

"I can read this word for word or just use plain English. You tell me," John announced.

"English," Matt said impatiently, not sparing a glance in her direction, "I've got a lot to do before sundown."

Perri calmly nodded her assent. He was going to have to work harder than that to provoke her this time.

"Okay," John began, "you both inherit the bulk of Gannie's estate and share the duties of co-executors. The acreage behind the house that borders the Ransoms' is left to Matt, up to but not including the horse barn. You split the oil royalties." He paused on a wry smile. "I figure that will keep you two tied up in paperwork with the oil companies for at least a year and a half.

"Perri gets the house and the surrounding acres, from the horse barn to the highway, including the graveyard." The attorney raised his eyes, as if to check and see how they were taking the fifty-fifty split. "And you both inherit this project of hers—the 'Donated Land' out on the lake. The money, accounts, etc., are divided equally, aside from some bequests listed on page two." Pages rustled as the inheritors followed along.

"If you would like extra copies, just let me know," he added. John's gaze lingered on Perri. "And, of course, I will be glad to send a copy on to your attorney in New York, Perri, if you like."

She returned the look calmly, certain he still couldn't reconcile in his mind the sophisticated businesswoman she had become with little Perri Stone. Something was going on. She could feel it. Only her abiding trust in John Deepwater and the certainty that Matt didn't know any more than she did, kept her from tensing up. It was arduous enough to hear John speak about the division of Gledhill. It just about broke her heart to think of it.

"It sounds pretty straightforward, for a piece of legal work," Matt remarked as he rapidly flipped pages. "But you don't seem too enthused, John. What is it?"

"Well, there's one hitch," John said calmly.

"Then let's hear it," Matt demanded.

That did it. "Oh, surely, Matt and I can work it out reasonably, John." Perri cast a reproachful glance at this stranger she had once known so well. "If there's something Gannie wanted us to do, I'm willing to make every effort."

"Yes, well, darlin'," John began easily, "what she wanted you to do was to marry Matt Ransom. If you decline, the land will be sold for condominiums."

Two

Ransom wasn't fooled. John Deepwater, Esq. was making a supreme effort not to smile as they absorbed the news. And allowing as how Deepwater's poker face was a legend in the county, he almost pulled it off.

It was a successful effort by Matt's estimation. But Matt had known John too long and too well. And what he knew of the man had him practically hovering over his chair, like a hawk just waiting for the field mouse to blink.

"Did she say why, in the blazes, she made our getting married a part of the deal?" Matt demanded in none too gentle tones. He felt Perri flinch at the word "married." Well, he could hardly blame the woman for that.

Deepwater took a deep breath. "She said she wanted to get your attention," he replied calmly. One would have thought little old ladies routinely made getting married a condition for inheriting their estates.

Well, Deepwater wasn't the only poker player in the room. No one would have known from his stoic, emotionless expression just how deeply the memory of Perri in that back bedroom at Gledhill was weighing down Matt's heart. Even though he was rocked by this latest development, he couldn't pull his mind back from the way she had felt in his arms just a few hours ago.

It was all he could do to sit there and ignore her. He couldn't get beyond the sight of Perri standing again in Gledhill. As if she had grown into a woman right here in Spirit, instead of a world away. He swore silently at the realization that he had sorely underestimated this woman. Just as he had obviously underestimated Gannie; and once, only once, his own late mother.

Yet again, he reminded himself of how wrong he had been to love Perri. He had shown such poor judgment in trusting her twelve years ago. For that, he no longer blamed Perri Stone. She had been too young; and Matt had repeated the same mistake after she'd gone. These days, he didn't have much time for women and he accepted that. It was in some ways a pity, because he genuinely did enjoy them. He just had nothing to give a woman but himself, the land and a lot of hard work.

He hadn't managed to do the one thing he had felt was his duty: To take care of those he loved. The fact that he still, after everything, wanted a family was something never examined. It felt almost shameful to want anything. The disastrous results of his own youthful pride had left him ashamed he still cared. And now, just about the only thing he had left was his own damn pride.

The silence stretched before Matt said quietly, "My attention or our attention?"

"She wanted both of you to pay attention," John clarified. "She figured the condition of you two either getting married or losing the land would make an impression."

Matt snorted and spared a glance for the woman seated at his side. Perri looked like she would run if she could just figure out how to go about it. It struck him solidly that if she did run this time, he would go after her.

It was a shock to discover how rapidly Perri Stone could sink back into his system. He didn't care for it. Matt clamped down hard on the urge to get mean twice in one day.

He had fully intended that kiss earlier to be antagonistic, maybe a little punishing. Matt had figured if he offended her just enough, she would keep her distance. That would be easier for all concerned. He really hadn't planned to make love to her mouth. He still wasn't entirely certain how that had happened.

A small portion of his brain puzzled over the fact that the taste of the woman could be so much more powerful than that of the girl she had been twelve years ago. He had loved that Perri with all his young heart.

Now the woman she had become summoned him on some deep level. That would never do. Matt would have sworn he could no longer feel anything that deeply and he had no intention of starting now. So it was back to business.

Deepwater went on talking. "The Ransoms and the Stones, and the Marlowes, through Perri here," he said nodding in her direction, "would be announcing that they were united in an attempt to bring some sort of new business into the area. The town would see a strong commitment, a strong front.

"As you know," John continued, "our parents and grandparents tried a couple of decades ago to position Spirit Valley for the future. But they made their efforts based upon Spirit as a continuing center of commerce." He paused briefly. "Nobody dreamed it would ever get like this. So nobody planned for the worst." John sighed. "They complacently expected things to continue as they had always been."

Perri finally spoke. "I think accusing them of complacency is a little harsh, John. Nobody could have predicted drought, the oil bust and the railroad's demise," she pointed out.

"Thank you, Miss Oklahoma Girl Stater," Matt interjected dryly, "but we're getting off the subject here." Didn't she realize her calm appeal for reason was killing him?

Perri remained unruffled and coolly crossed her legs. He realized he was staring. He realized she knew it. How she could remain that placid was just beyond him. He made a mental note to set about breaking down that composed demeanor at the first opportunity.

Matt grimly turned his attention back to the man he was be-

ginning to think of as "that lawyer." "I want to know what
Gannie said," Matt demanded. "Why did she want me to marry
Stone here? And, Johnnie, don't you give me that attorney/client
confidentiality crap."

John Deepwater looked his best friend in the eye. "She said
it was time you did something you should have done over ten
years ago."

Perri inhaled sharply. John continued. "She said it was time
that the Stone-Ransom animosity was put to rest for the good of
all concerned. Now that you're both older. Now that…you're
both single, Gannie felt it was high time you two got married."
He didn't have to add, "now that Leila Ransom is dead." The
words John left unspoken were a silent outcry heard by everyone
in the room.

"But why?" Perri spoke so low she might have been alone.
"Why barter me and buy him? I have no interest in holding Matt
to anything he said twelve years ago. As a matter of fact," she
continued, "I'm grateful to him for ending it. I was way too
young to get married. Please tell me why she would do this,
Johnnie."

Matt was saved from responding to that bit about her being
"grateful" when he saw Deepwater's face gentle into a faint
smile. As always, it softened the fierceness of his features to a
surprising degree.

"Gannie said she promised your grandmother Anne to always
look out for you and your mother." Matt and Perri both displayed a momentary lack of composure at the mention of Perri's
grandmother, Anne. "She said it was time for the Stone/Marlowe
women to stop running—that you, in particular, needed to come
home. That even later," he added, "and divorced from Matt,
you'd be accepted as a member of the community and not as an
outsider. She said: 'Perri needs to have her home restored. The
Ransoms took it from her and they can damn well give it back.'"

Matt sat silently, his mind racing around all the angles as John
continued. "So folks, here's the bottom line. Number one, you
two have ninety days to accept or decline the terms of the will.
If you marry, you stay married for at least six months before

entertaining the possibility of a divorce—all the while, you must live together in the Gledhill place.''

Matt stirred indignantly at that. "I don't have the time to be driving back and forth to the farm," he said. "I've got horses to see to. I've—"

"Oh, please. It's down the road, not even a mile," Perri interjected. "I live 2,000-something miles away and you have the nerve to whine about how—"

"Number two," Deepwater's rich, courtroom voice filled the little office. "You come up with a plan to use the land she's donated to Spirit in a way that will benefit the area. From the way she described it to me, what she wanted from y'all..."

John's eyes were drawn to a photograph on the wall behind his clients' chairs. His voice trailed off. Matt could almost feel him looking back to a time before the sound of the starting gun for the Run of '89. The day the town of Spirit Valley sprung up overnight.

"Well," John continued, "it was as if she wanted you two to homestead and make the improvements necessary to maintain a claim. I think that's how she saw it, as a claim. I think it was important to her that the two of you were the ones to find some way to bring people and commerce into the area." John looked from Perri to Matt, letting his words sink in.

"But I don't want to bring people into the area," Matt pointed out politely. "I want them to stay out."

"Well, then you're going to have them in your lap, Matt," his friend replied just as politely as you please. "The house and the land will be sold to the developers and you'll have a condominium resting up by your east pasture." The thought of that left all three of them breathless.

"Gary Kell is the attorney for the developers and he is just about beside himself, he wants that deal so bad," John stated grimly. "So unless you put your back into this project, not only will you lose the inheritance of that land, you're going to have people just about up your nose.

"Perri," John continued, "I've seen the plans. They are trying to be sensitive and tasteful about it, but the condo will surround the old graveyard. Some of your family is buried there.''

Perri looked away.

"Of course, maybe that's your preference," he added with studied carelessness.

Well, *that* brought her head back around to stare him down. The tears in her eyes had dried in an instant and the green glints flashed with a renewed show of spirit.

Good, Matt thought. Whatever else had happened, the woman had acquired some grit along the way.

"Take the money," John continued in the same indifferent vein, "and let us become even more of a bedroom community for Oklahoma City than we already are."

"So, is that all?" The simmer and sizzle of Ransom's slow burn could probably be detected all the way *to* Oklahoma City.

"No." Deepwater replied soberly. "No."

"Well?" Matt was in no mood to be strung along. And he still wasn't fooled. John had been looking forward to this. "What else did she say?"

Deepwater's gaze fell upon Perri. "She said 'Tell Perri I said it was time she stopped running and came home.'" Perri looked deeply into John's eyes, as if she were trying to see Gannie's face emerge from their onyxlike surface. "'Tell her I said for her to just trust me.'"

"Don't make me drag it out of you, John. What else?" Matt demanded.

A surprisingly boyish grin lit Deepwater's face as he looked at Ransom. "She said: 'And Johnnie, when Matthew starts to squawk, you just tell him he should have paid more attention. Back when I was trying to teach him how to play chess.'"

Just trust me.

Out in the parking lot, Perri fumbled with the car keys and the copies of Gannie's will. She had excused herself and gotten out quick. From the look of the sky, Spirit was caught between two opposing weather patterns, one to the north, the other to the east. The light had turned that clear, lovely shade of pale, apple green that Perri associated with soon-to-follow destructive weather.

The weather had been as good an excuse as any to make a graceful exit. The ex-Mrs. Gary Kell, the lovely Lida, had been lying in wait in the outer office when the three of them had emerged. She had immediately draped herself all over Matt like a cheap suit, the better to pump him for details. It took a stronger stomach than Perri had possessed at the moment to witness that.

Strong wind blew her hair into her eyes as she tried to get it straight which key on the unfamiliar ring fit the car door. A large, bronzed hand took the ring from her, inserting the proper key and holding open the door. "Thank you, Matt," she said formally.

He was wearing a suit, his hair just curling around the collar of his shirt. And cologne. She could sort of halfway deal with him when he was in boots and jeans, but not in a suit. Perri fought the urge to hang her head and not look at the man. He looked too good, too solid, his presence too comforting.

"I've asked John to dig out whatever boilerplate he's got on hand for prenuptial agreements," Matt said. "You have an appointment tomorrow morning at 9 a.m., right after mine," he added rapidly upon her glare, "for a medical checkup."

Jolted out of the notion of a "comforting" Matt Ransom, Perri stared at him. *"What?"* she cried.

"Doc Berkka is leaving for Tenkiller," Matt said as if that settled it.

It did. "Of course. Silly me," she said dryly. "Whatever was I thinking?"

Trips to the lake were sacred to the Berkkas. Back when the current Dr. Berkka's grandfather was in practice, every cesarean birth in June had been scheduled to accommodate the fish.

"So, do we sign a prenup?" Matt demanded. "Book the church? Get a jump on the next thing that lawyer is going to tell us to do?"

She had to ask. "Just when did Johnnie Deepwater become 'that lawyer'?"

"When he told me I had to marry you, that's when," Matt roared.

Perri's face tilted up toward his as they squared off. "Thank you so very much for announcing that at the top of your lungs," she answered. "We can finish the job if you go on over to Blue's Tavern. I'll head for Marjorie's Beauty Shop and then the whole damn county will be up to date on our personal affairs by sundown."

"Now who's shouting?"

"Go to hell, Ransom," she said sweetly.

For a moment he simply looked at her as the wind brutally lashed at them both. "Hell is where I've lived for the last twelve years."

Perri marched back through Gannie's front door, past her cousin LaDonna Marlowe, and headed right for the wine.

"The storm's moved on to Apache, now that you've got your stuff out of my place during the worst of it. I brought beer," Donnie called absently from the couch as she removed the cotton separating each newly painted pink toenail.

"I knew better than to bring food, what with all the casseroles. Want one? A beer, I mean," she clarified, looking up from her toes. "No, I guess you don't." Donnie watched with cautious fascination as Perri dumped her purse, slapped her copies of the will down on the sideboard, filled a goblet with wine and threw back a big swallow. Huge, blue eyes got even bigger. "What?" she demanded. "Tell me."

"I have ninety days to decide to marry Matt Ransom and keep this place intact," Perri announced. "Or, I can decline marriage to that particular prince of darkness and see Gledhill sold out from under me for condominiums."

The silence lengthened as Donnie took in her cousin's words. "Oh, I am nowhere near drunk enough for you to be telling me this," Donnie replied. "I just started on this beer. Now slowly, and from the top."

Perri repeated the full exchange in Deepwater's office. "Eek," Donnie said weakly.

"Maybe I won't have to make this decision," Perri continued. "Maybe Matt will refuse and I won't have to make any kind of a choice about the land."

Her voice trailed off at the sound of a vehicle moving hard up the drive. On a sigh, they both braced themselves and, taking a sip, set goblet and beer bottle aside. There was no choice when it came to Matt or to the land. It didn't need saying.

"Donnie," Matt nodded at the little brunette upon entering the living room. He paused to consider her screaming pink toenails. "Does the county sheriff's office know what its 'star' deputy is wearing underneath her uniform?" he demanded.

"Matt." Donnie gave him a luminous smile that said: 'I ain't movin.'

He looks dangerous; ready to blow, Perri thought as she glanced toward the woman she loved like a sister. The tension in the room made it difficult to maintain the appearance of nonchalance. Donnie would manage it somehow, Perri was certain. This was too good not to watch them play it out.

A train whistled softly past the crossing and into the distance as Perri's stance widened to mirror Matt's own. Both of them had their weight transferred to the balls of their feet. They were poised like two gunslingers facing off.

The only sounds were the ever-present wind, and the ticking of the clock on the mantel. Tread lightly, Matt, Perri silently cautioned. No matter what, he was going to have to work a bit harder to wear her down than he'd done twelve years ago.

"We didn't finish our conversation before you ran off," he said. "Again."

"On the contrary," she answered, "there's nothing more to say for the moment, Matt."

"You still haven't said yes or no, Stone," he challenged.

"No, I haven't," she shot back, "and I don't intend to. Yet. I have ninety days before the decision is due."

Did he have to look that great? Why couldn't he be an out-of-shape, doughy accountant, for heaven's sake? And *why* had those adorable dimples of his sharpened into such a dangerous face? It really wasn't fair, damn him.

"Ninety days?" Matt echoed as he slowly covered the distance between them. "If you plan to string me along for three months, think again."

"I don't plan to 'string you along' at all," she countered. "But I won't be pressured into a snap decision either." She stood her ground and took a deep breath. "I want to at least sleep on it, Matt. So should you." Perri tilted her head to look up with steady eyes as he reached the end of his walk. He didn't have to know how much it cost her. "Am I to conclude from this unexpected visit that you *want* us to get married?" she asked dryly.

Matt looked again at Donnie as if she'd missed her cue. "Forget it," she said flatly.

"Donnie." Perri smiled, never taking her eyes off Matt.

"Oh, all right." Donnie stood up carefully, like a woman unconvinced that her polish was completely dry. "But if you hurt her, Matt, I'll have to shoot you," she muttered, turning toward the hall. "I'll be in the kitchen," she stated unnecessarily and did the only sane thing a woman could do under the circumstances. She walked out on her heels.

"Okay, bottom line," Matt declared as they heard Donnie slap through the kitchen's swinging doors. "Gannie must have felt strongly about it if she wanted us to get married this badly. And she was right. The Ransoms, or at least *this* Ransom, should make the effort to restore your place in the community. And to restore your home."

Well, that answered that. Perri knew she might regret it, but she let him take her hand. His callused fingers rasped gently against the center of her palm. She couldn't help being drawn to him. It was all too well-known.

"Perri, I'm asking you to marry me." His smile was so sad and awkward, it affected her like a blow.

"I know this is a different marriage proposal than the last one you got from me." Restless, he turned away and moved to the mantel. His fingers automatically searched out the arrowhead he'd found one day, a lifetime ago. "It certainly will be a different marriage than the one I wanted with you," he acknowledged. "But I'm serious about it." His gaze remained on her

face as he gripped the thin, lethal piece of tapered stone. "So if there is another man in your life, tell me now," he demanded.

There was a long pause while she tried to get her breath. "But, we don't know each other anymore. I'm not sure I even like you," Perri continued with a calm totally at odds with how she felt. "And more to the point—is there a woman here in Spirit with certain expectations regarding her relationship with you?" she asked.

He gave her a blank look. She tried again. "Is there someone who would be hurt by our getting married, Matt?" Besides myself, she wondered.

Matt studied her, his eyes searching her face and body like he'd never seen her before. Suddenly he relaxed as if he'd reached a decision. Obviously, he wasn't listening to a word she'd said. And here she was, knocking herself out to be calm, reasonable and mature.

"I'm not involved with anyone myself, at the moment, but that is not the issue." She was going to maintain her dignity if it killed her. "If we go through with this—"

"No, there's no one," he said absently as he strolled back toward her. "And you're wrong about one thing. Who you're 'involved' with is most decidedly my business, as of now."

"But you've made it clear that you don't think much of me," she looked at him in bewilderment and quickly stifled another nervous urge to yawn. Could he be any more annoying? she wondered. Knowing him, she was soon to find out.

"That's not exactly true," he muttered gracelessly.

Where was this leading? It was best to keep it just business if she wanted to live through it. "All right. Let's just leave it," she said briskly, getting a grip on her heart. She shook off the hopes and dreams of a past that was bygone.

"If this is your idea of down-home charm, it's not working." She paused and coolly looked him over. "And I can't help but wonder if you knew about the conditions of the will in advance. You didn't seem all that shocked over the idea of a marriage. Were you just getting a charge out of toying with me earlier today?" she demanded.

The skin around those cheekbones seemed to tighten at her words. "You used to be such a sweet little girl," he said in furious tones.

"But that doesn't mean I was stupid." She couldn't quite keep the smile out of her voice. Apparently Mr. Ransom was not best pleased by the question.

"I may have been a little girl, but I was at least smart enough to be in love with a decent young man. One, I might add, who was honorable enough to propose marriage and mean it." Perri stared out the window at the nearby tree as a breeze played lightly through the leaves. Just as it had always done. It helped her get hold of herself.

"Yeah, I suppose I was a sweet little girl," she sighed, the threat of tears receding. How could he make her want to cry and then smile in the spin of a dime? How could he make her want something that no longer existed with such reckless intensity? A recklessness that fully acknowledged how much it would hurt six months down the road. "I will think about the idea of marrying you and see if I can live with it," she said formally. "I'll get back to you in a day or two."

He chuckled as if he was actually beginning to enjoy that snippy tone. "Come here," he said softly, holding out his arms. She hesitated before walking into his light embrace. "I'm sorry I worked so hard to get your goat earlier. And no, I didn't know she had marriage in mind for us. I would have promised, at least to look out for you," he admitted grudgingly, "if she'd asked. Truce?" His lips lightly played along her temple.

Perri relaxed slightly and smiled. "Truce," she said.

"Good," Matt murmured as he smoothed her hair from her shoulders. Without warning he skillfully covered her mouth with his. There was a moment when she all but tasted his frustration. Then she felt him let it go as he deepened the kiss. The tender quality changed everything.

He overwhelmed her common sense and left her totally unprepared for the sudden transfer into sweetness. His kiss became a gentle appeal rather than an angry demand and the effect was shattering. She gave more of herself than ever before.

Never had she wanted a man the way she wanted Matt at this moment. The tenderness contained such a quality of honesty between them, it almost brought tears to her eyes. She clung to his jacket and found a depth of feeling she could never have envisioned with him. Even young Matt hadn't stirred her so acutely.

The kiss intensified and changed. His hands began to move over her, molding her to him, keeping her close. They roamed down to her hips, his thumbs playing over her protruding hipbones before he tilted her pelvis into him. She rose up to cradle his aroused flesh.

His hand traveled up to her breast. She arched into him as his thumb found her nipple already erect. "I'm going to have you, Perri," he said softly as he lay openmouthed kisses against her throat and jaw. "We're going to have each other and at least some kind of a marriage," he vowed, "unless you can look me in the eye and tell me 'no' like you mean it."

He kissed her deeply, as if they had all the time in the world. Perri's bones were melting as she clung to him. The mood shifted again and became more demanding. She felt herself straining toward Matt when he abruptly pulled back from the kiss.

"Now that we've got a truce," he said, breathing hard, "let me state my plans." His grip moved from her shoulders to her nape, his thumbs supporting her jaw, as he kissed her hard and fast. "You may not have heard, darlin'," he said, "but I've been slap out of tact for some time, so I'll be direct.

"We've got ninety days," he reminded her. "I plan to see to it that each one is an exercise in sheer torment until you say 'Yes, Matt, I'll be pleased to be your wife.' We are going to honor Gannie's wishes, Per," he went on. "Even though the word 'honor' just about sticks in my throat..."

That did it. Fury lashed apart the sexy haze he'd led her toward. Perri was well and truly riled. His words and the fact that he had kissed her right out of all reason and into a stupor were too much. She started to haul off and hit him, but he had always been too quick.

Matt grabbed her and pulled her up off her feet, so that they were eye-to-eye. "I asked you nicely first," he reminded her.

His tone hardened. "Now, I'm telling you. Get ready for a wedding, 'cause you are getting married. I'm not going to let anything or anybody build a damn condo on this property," he vowed. "And if, by some screwup, you are responsible for such a thing ever rising out of Gledhill, I will personally take some long and very painful strips right out of your pretty hide.

"And understand this," he added with grim determination. "I plan to see to it, Ms. Stone, that you're my wife in every sense of the word." He set her down sharply.

"You can say 'yes' now or spend the next three months looking over your shoulder," Matt called loudly after her as she pushed past him and headed for the kitchen. "It's up to you."

"Miss Marlowe," he called out with a little too much glee. The look on Perri's face as she stalked into the kitchen had Donnie moving through the swinging doors looking for a fight. "Try to explain to your cousin from New York that it's a done deal.

"And," he added as he walked to the door, "please tell Ms. Stone, I'll see her in church." He graciously closed the front door behind him on a grim little smile.

Donnie returned to the kitchen to find her cousin leaning up against the counter. Navy blue eyes narrowed, wincing as Perri gently banged her forehead, just once, against the kitchen cabinet.

"Well, nobody can accuse that man of a lack of intensity," Donnie announced.

"Nobody can accuse him of having a soul either," Perri muttered. She slowly pushed back from the counter and tried to get a rein on her temper.

Only now did she notice she was holding the arrowhead in a viselike grip, with no notion of when he had put it into her hand. She looked down at her palm. Perri had squeezed the implement of war hard enough for the sharp edges to leave marks.

Donnie stood patiently for a time, waiting for the storm to pass. "Shall I heat up one of the casseroles the church ladies landed on us, while you get out of that suit?"

Perri sighed and turned to the little brunette. "Why stop at one?" she asked.

* * *

Matt passed his own place and kept going. He needed a minute or two to calm down. The lake, he thought as he tore at his tie. I'll just stop off for a minute at the lake. It wasn't far and the sight of all that water never failed to soothe him.

He veered off the road to the main picnic area and away from the skiers, making for a secluded section where he had a better chance for a moment of peace. It was a mistake.

He had taken Perri here. He had told her he loved her and wanted to marry her right about where he was now parked. He slammed out of the car and looked around rather wildly at where he had just driven himself, in his own vehicle, by his own hand. "Just shoot me," he muttered.

She had tasted lightly of wine, he thought. It had only served to enhance the well-remembered taste of her. Matt wanted her. After all this time, and to the point of violence. The feelings of tenderness, laced with shots of fury had him off balance. If she had been appealing to him before, she was devastating now. His hands fisted as he could almost feel her hair brush through his fingers. Matt swore to himself.

How could he explain to Perri that she was no longer the true source of his anger, but instead a painful reminder of his own dreadful mistakes? Pride made it all but impossible to acknowledge the need he now felt for the woman Perri had become without him. A woman he just knew was going to leave.

Ransoms didn't leave. They stayed. They remained anchored to the land; ever since 1891, when a spinster schoolteacher had taken in a half-breed foundling and raised him for her own.

Miss Vienna Whitaker, obviously Southern and a lady to her fingertips, had named the baby Matthew Lawrence, after her beloved father. But for reasons unknown, Miss Vienna had given the child the last name of Ransom.

The citizens of Spirit Valley could only speculate as to why she had chosen the name. Some thought it a good name. With no one in Indian Territory named Ransom, no one could be blamed for having fathered a half-Indian baby.

Those citizens with a dictionary alongside the family Bible, had puzzled over what the ransom was for. If raising the child was the price of atonement, then what was the sin? And whose, exactly? Miss Vienna hadn't seen fit to share her reasoning. She had quietly raised a fine son, who later became a much-respected member of the community.

Like his father, Sam, Matt didn't give much thought to the source of their need to take care of what his great-great-grandfather had been given. Nor did he give any thought to his automatic mistrust for those who moved on. Its origins were as deeply engrained as the desire to maintain a well-respected position in the community. His folks had always stayed, spit in the dust and stuck it out.

No, Ransoms didn't leave, they were too busy. None had shirked the responsibility of family and land. None, that is, except for one. Matt's grandfather, Lawrence Ransom, had done just that when he had run off with Anne Marlowe, the grandmother of Perri Stone.

Since that time everything had changed. It certainly had stained Matt's love for Perri. As soon as Matt had declared his intention to make Perri his wife, everything he had subsequently put his heart into had turned to dust. Even later on when his brother had drifted off, the unspoken assumption had been that somehow the wounds of the past had caused Whit to leave town as soon as he was able. But the violence and scandal their grandparents had launched was not Perri's fault. It shamed him to think he couldn't rise above that one fact. Matt noticed that it evoked interest to realize that he still could feel a sense of shame about anything.

He wished he could muster up some feelings for the way he had treated Perri twelve years ago. But they were locked in ice. Matt had wanted to destroy her that night. He speculated now on just how close he had come to achieving his goal.

Once Sam had stormed out of the house that night, Leila had laid it on thick about the old scandal. Then as if his grandparents hadn't been reason enough, she had told him his father was keeping Janie Stone—Perri's mother—as his mistress. Matt's attempts to reason with her had only served to make his mother more lethal.

Today, his own youthful arrogance and naiveté astounded him. He had foolishly assumed his parents' objections would be due to Perri's age; and he had been preparing his argument for some time along that line. He knew now that he had underestimated his mother as a fighter. But then, he had never gone up against anyone like her.

The force of her rage had been terrifying. And underneath the emotions, what she had said had made some sense. His mother had made it plain that Perri Stone couldn't possibly love a Ransom. After all, since Perri was aware of Sam's involvement with Janie, then her eagerness to marry Matt had to be founded on a desire to exact some small degree of revenge on the Ransoms. If Perri had truly loved him, Leila had made it clear that Marlowe honor would have demanded Perri let Matt go.

Looking back on it, his actions later that night had been due as much to the way Leila had aroused his emotions as to what she had actually said to him. He had left a sobbing Leila and gone for a much-needed drive to cool off. He hadn't wanted to go directly to Gledhill and have it out with a seventeen-year-old girl who loved him. But by the time Matt did show up, he hadn't been able to calm his fury over his mother's accusations.

He could still see Perri in the darkened living room, looking paralyzed with shame and fear. It only now occurred to him that he had never asked her what that was about. He'd never taken a moment to find out if something was wrong. He had just started in and said some appalling things to her.

When she had denied his mother's accusations about his dad and Janie, he had nearly lost it. He quite simply hadn't believed her. After all, she had seemed to expect his indictment.

"He hasn't been seeing my mother," Perri had all but screamed. "She's not seeing anybody."

"Of course," Matt had whispered, gently touching her cheek. She had such smooth skin. He had scared her with that gentle stroke. But still Perri had hung on to her lies. Just as his mother had predicted she would. "You've got good reason to think I'm stupid enough to believe you. Don't you, baby?" he had asked softly. "You've gone all the way to convince me, haven't you?"

Matt winced when he thought of how he had roped the chain of the gold locket around one hand and grabbed her shoulder with the other. His fingers had dug in as he had pulled her to him. Perri's eyes had dilated in shock at his savage behavior.

He had given her the necklace as a symbol of their secret engagement, until the time was right for a ring and a formal announcement. That night, he had struggled not to rip it from her throat. The heavy snake chain had held, but he knew the contempt in his eyes had destroyed her where she stood. Still, Perri had said nothing. She hadn't tried to defend herself, only her mother.

"I'm real impressed," he'd said. "You're good, I'll give you that." He had roughly pushed her away and headed out the door. Matt's last memory of Perri was a glimpse of her through the window, trying to rub away the red marks already forming on her throat.

From that night on, his pride had focused on his role in maintaining a respected position in the community. He had set himself apart from his father and younger brother to see that scandal didn't touch another generation of Ransoms.

And it was more than his relationship with Perri that hadn't survived that night. To this day, his relationship with his father was forever altered as well. They worked together and lived on the same property, but boundary lines had been drawn by Matt's resulting sense of betrayal.

Matt idly watched a very fat blue jay repeatedly dive-bomb a squirrel. That brought him back to the present. It dawned on him, as he looked around, that he'd never brought Cadie out here during their brief marriage. He'd never brought his wife to a place he considered so important, so much his. Never shared it with her. He couldn't. This spot was forever associated with memories of Perri.

He felt the fury drain away as he accepted that he wanted her. He wanted Perri with a single-mindedness of purpose that sooner or later would leave his heart on the line. He'd just have to find a way around the fact that Perri Stone was settling back into his blood and soul with an ease he wouldn't have thought possible.

Matt couldn't trust himself to take the best road for either of them. Hurting her again would most likely hurt him down to the ground. But for the life of him he couldn't stop himself from behavior that was bound to cause them both sorrow.

How many more times was he going to hurt Perri Stone? The same woman he had once wanted to protect for a lifetime? How many times now had he attempted deliverance, some sort of atonement? Hadn't that been the real reason he had married Cadie?

After Perri left, he had married a sweet, fragile girl who had needed him to take care of her. Matt laughed ruefully. Leila had secretly despised Cadie as much as she had Perri, maybe more. It had really killed Leila not to be able to call upon Cadie's honor as a tool for manipulation. Cadie hadn't understood honor. All she had understood was competing.

What *he* hadn't understood at the time was that he had been the prize. His own willful pride hadn't let him see that simple fact. He had been so sure life was never going to break Matt Ransom. So convinced that life would have to bend, not himself. He got back in his car and started for home.

All Cadie had wanted was to get married to someone "better" than either of her sisters and have a baby. She had had no plan, no thought about what would happen after that. She had not been prepared for a reality beyond the point where she would reach her goal. So when she had miscarried the second time, to her it was as if she'd lost everything.

Cadie had gotten in the car one day, shortly after being released from the hospital, and headed west. She hadn't given herself time to heal. If Matt could have done something for her, she hadn't let him know what it was.

Funny about that. She had zeroed in early and locked onto his need to take care of his family, to have children to carry on for the land. Well, he had failed at all of that and now he'd had a bellyful of women who needed someone to take care of them.

Near Tucumcari, New Mexico, she had been killed by a drunk driver during a sudden, violent storm. Cadie had pulled over, seeking the protection of an overpass and had been plowed right into the concrete wall. Bad luck. Sorry for your loss, Ransom.

It had left him wild, mean with grief. But Gannie had turned Matt around. She had never been afraid of his rage. Gannie was someone who could love him and would stay during the hard times. He hadn't managed to drive her away. God, he missed her more than he did his dead wife and his mother combined. He steered the car away from the lake.

Good thing for Perri that she bugged out when she did, he thought. No, it hadn't been Perri's fault. Bad luck. Sorry for your loss, you sorry fool.

And so he had grieved, finally. Thanks to Gannie, he hadn't had to do it alone. Matt reckoned that maybe being the one left behind at home to deal with broken dreams hadn't changed him too much for the worse.

If not, it was thanks to Gannie. He grinned in spite of everything. Matt didn't think Gannie would be too proud of his behavior today. He knew he wasn't. *I'm not much impressed with your attitude, Matthew.* He could just hear her now.

He'd gone out of his way today to needle Perri. He had meant to keep it up until he had gotten a response from her other than that cool-handed, white-gloved crap. He had had to make her lose her composure, just to prove to himself she was not as immune to him as she had seemed.

And he had been so sure he could bully her into bending to his will; into doing what had to be done. He hadn't even thought through how she might stand and take it instead. And how that might hurt her. His reasoning had centered on how she had faded away without a fight twelve years before. Well, obviously, that was twelve years gone.

He shouldn't have taken it as far as he had today. He had to work with the woman. He had to cooperate with her in order to get a job done and it wasn't going to be easy now that he had kissed her.

She had every right to be furious with him, and hurt. He had been out of line to call her honor into question like that. Gledhill meant as much to Perri as it did to him and he knew it. And on top of that, Matt's own fury, fueled by an ever-present despair, had caused him to screw up even that, what had been the first moment of real tenderness he had felt in a long, lonely time.

He turned into the drive toward his home. As he drove under the wrought-iron arch, announcing to anyone passing by that this was Ransom Horse Farm, a Cadillac and a Lincoln pulled in behind him. Matt steeled himself to be cordial to the arriving owners and mentally rehearsed what he had to say about their horses.

For the time being, thoughts of exactly how in the hell he was going to persuade Perri Stone to marry him, and marry him now, were pushed aside in favor of the business at hand.

Three

"**I** know you're not thrilled to hear this, but I'm glad Matt talked you into getting married," Donnie announced, as she turned off Route 66 toward old Fort Remount.

"He didn't talk me into it. The land did," Perri replied softly. Actually, she reflected, a sunset had been responsible for her decision. A few days after the reading of the will, she had gone to sit on Gledhill's back porch and watch the nightly display.

With a horse nickering softly somewhere nearby, Perri had sipped at her wine, as the jet stream had worked its way through the dazzling colors of the setting sun. As she drank in its beauty, the consequences of not marrying Matt had become very clear. If she couldn't bring herself to do it, she would lose the colors of the sunset on the hill.

What does one do with an inheritance? Perri mused as she stared out the car window. She didn't kid herself. Families were often ripped to shreds by the wrong caretaker being placed in command. Aside from its outlaw status, Oklahoma had been founded on the blood and the bones of who had been allotted what.

Perri wondered if, with this marriage, she was about to lose that part of herself she had so carefully pasted back together. Events were moving too fast to sense right action from wrong, good from bad.

She took a deep breath and tried for honesty. Perri acknowledged what she hadn't been able to actually come out and say— to herself, much less to him. She didn't want the marriage to end when their six months were up. It was burdensome to admit that she still wanted a real marriage with Matt, especially when it seemed he was hell-bent on driving her away.

Yet she would marry him, no matter how it pained her. She wouldn't be responsible for losing Gledhill. Perri noted with mild interest that she now felt a familiar anguish. It twined itself around the practice of running away from what she loved, in order to hang onto herself.

Now she had something outside herself, from which she wouldn't run. But she still had to find a way to take a stand and not permit herself to be beaten down by the circumstances.

"The land," she whispered as they continued along the stately drive. Matt had acted as if she'd needed instruction into what it meant.

"This life isn't for everyone, sweetheart," he had said on one of his daily attempts to wear her down. "It's too hard for some. It will probably break your heart if you love it. Worse, it can break your spirit. For even if you love the land with all of your heart, blood and bones, that may not be enough."

She had taken a good look into her heart before answering. In that one moment, she had known she was going to stay for good. "I agree with you, Matt," she'd answered. "Loving this place isn't enough. Sentimentality won't cut it. The land has to love you and want you to stay." She had studied him for a quiet moment. "Isn't it an act of faith on both sides?" she'd asked. And she had agreed to marry him.

"Well, I never figured you for a June bride, much less Matt Ransom's June bride," Donnie's remark broke into her thoughts. "And Lord knows, you barely squeaked under the wire. But honey, you do look stunning in that dress. It was the right choice," she said smiling.

The fluid, draped neckline and three-quarter-length sleeves set the tone for ease and understatement. By necessity, the ivory sheath was also cool and comfortable. This was going to be a get-in-get-out kind of wedding, with no music but that of the wind through the trees.

Perri grimly arched an eyebrow. Her maid of honor was being just a little too sweet. "Excuse me," she said politely, "but shopping with you for this dress was hell. I'd rather be forced to participate in the annual rattlesnake roundup than go through that again. You," she reminded her driver, "are the one who, when I pointed out that I needed something to go with the church, said: 'What will go with that church is calico and a stovepipe bonnet.'"

"Well," Donnie replied a little defensively, "what else goes with a hundred-and-something-year-old adobe church? That Givenchy suit you were trying on at the time made you look like a junior officer for the Star Fleet Federation."

"It's not easy finding the appropriate dress for a marriage of convenience," Perri said through gritted teeth.

"I don't know why you keep calling it that," Donnie replied. "So far, there's been nothing 'convenient' about it." After the last three weeks, Donnie had made it clear that remaining an old maid was looking real good.

Perri turned her attention back to the old Army outpost as they continued toward the heart of the fort. It had been settled shortly after the Civil War, long before any settlers had arrived. The 4th Cavalry and their Indian scouts were buried in the cemetery, having died in battles mainly with the Northern Cheyenne. Perri was struck by the recent work that had gone into restoring the grasses to the way they had been over a hundred years ago. Without warning, sapphire blue water caught her eye. "Stop a second, Donnie," she abruptly requested.

Donnie slowed, pulled over and turned to her cousin. "Please, do not tell me that you are getting cold feet," she declared. "I left my gun at home. It doesn't go with this dress."

"No, look." Perri's eyes drank in the sight of a snow-white egret resting near a pond of the only clear, blue water she had seen since her arrival. "Oh, God," she said dabbing at her eyes. "I can't cry now, and not over a pretty little pond."

Donnie took a deep breath and fumbled for a tissue. "Will you please stop it. I really don't want to cry and drive."

Perri remained silent for some time. She looked lovingly at the elms gracefully lining the drive. *Ready or not,* she thought. "Okay," she said quietly. "Let's get it done."

The silence. That was the dominant feature of Fort Remount. There was no other sound but the wind. Matt stood under an elm, drinking in the sight of a forgotten piece of history. It was probably every boy's fantasy come true. An old Indian outpost that hadn't been altered much in over a hundred years, it was at this point almost deserted.

Fort Remount's church wasn't much bigger than a postage stamp, he observed. As befitted a remount outpost, its stables had been its heart. Any religion had probably centered on a funeral service or a quick prayer for Godspeed through hostile territory.

Good thing it was a small wedding, and a fast one. Even if the stucco walls kept it cool, even if amber glass windows made the cherry-wood pews glow. The little building wasn't air-conditioned. But Perri had absolutely refused to marry him in their church in town. He hadn't challenged her on it. Sam had married Leila in that church, and Matt had married Cadie there.

Matt turned his thoughts back to the memory of Perri's grim acceptance of his proposal. "I'm going shopping tomorrow for a wedding dress," she'd said. "John will call you with the details of when and where you are to show up and say 'I do.' Try to have the cows fed and the horses watered so you can make it on time. And if you have any notion of bringing a date to the wedding," she'd added dryly, "keep in mind it was Gannie who taught me how to shoot." And so, here he stood, ready or not.

A lean, middle-aged man walked around to open the car door for his passenger. Janie Stone gracefully got out of the car. Sam Ransom had insisted on driving to Oklahoma City to pick up the mother of the bride.

Like Matt and John Deepwater, Sam had gotten out of his car in his best Stetson, suit and boots. Each of the men quietly commanded, rather than demanded attention, in an individual manner that somehow coalesced into a statement of unity, adding quiet honor to the wedding taking place that day under a blue Oklahoma sky.

Matt noted that Janie seemed cautious around Sam; determined to maintain stringent boundaries. He came to attention with the sudden realization that his father still loved Janie Marlowe Stone. He watched carefully as Sam took great care with Perri's mother. And it was easy to see where Perri had gotten those legs.

Matt smiled as he watched Perri and Donnie arrive and go to her. The three women turned toward the little church and picked their way gracefully across the gravel with an identical thoroughbred gait.

She looks like spring; like new possibilities, Matt thought, suddenly on red alert. Perri looked so right to him. The plain, simple dress wasn't showy, wasn't tight and didn't advertise that there was a rather spectacular body underneath.

Deepwater seemed pensive as he watched Perri's ascent up the steps. "I don't recall her being filled out quite like that." He looked at Matt. "Do you?" he asked.

"Don't make me have to hit you, John," Matt said quietly to his best man. His eyes never left Perri. Lust hit him hard and unexpectedly.

Deepwater made a stab at looking innocent.

Thoughts of the night before had Matt smiling. He had gone over to Gledhill just to annoy her. Perri had been relaxing in the hot tub Gannie had installed on the glass-enclosed back porch. She had been in the nude. Of course he hadn't bothered to knock before strolling in the back door.

"You look relaxed," he'd said. She had looked anything but. He had been greatly amused by the fact that she'd clutched a magazine to her breasts upon his entry. "What are you reading?" he had asked innocently, "Bride Magazine?" That had caused a flash of annoyance in those pretty eyes.

"A computer software magazine," she'd replied, enunciating each word. "For systems and information technology professionals." She had almost removed it from her breasts to show him.

He had been quite pleased to see her so rattled. A devilish smile had reached his eyes. "Well, it looks real cute the way you're holding it, Perri," he'd said. "But it's pretty useless as a cover-up. And I do like what I see."

Matt had flat-out grinned as he'd stood leaning over the edge of the tub, making no effort to disguise his interest. Finally, he had pulled something out of his shirt pocket and straightened up. "I'll just leave this over here where it won't get wet," he had remarked casually, placing a small, gift-wrapped package on the table next to her.

"What is it?" Perri had eyed the package suspiciously, her magazine wet and disintegrating. Matt had stalked back toward her, a predator thoroughly amused by the prey's dilemma. He had leaned back over the edge of the tub. "A present for the bride," he'd said as his hand moved like lightning to the back of her neck. He'd kissed her long and hard, holding her head between his big hands, his tongue demanding the warmth of her mouth.

It hadn't been nice. It hadn't been gentle or sweet. It had been a voluptuous kiss that had made his impending intentions quite clear. Slowly he'd released her. "See you in church," he'd called over his shoulder as he'd moseyed out the back door. He had headed for his own side of the fence before she'd gotten the chance to unwrap those earrings. Before she'd had time to notice that he'd been as stiff as a board.

Matt knew he'd really pushed the envelope. He knew he didn't care. He enjoyed ticking her off. She was going to complain the gift was too extravagant. It was. And the minute he had seen those earrings, he had known they were for Perri.

But then, she was really going to have a fit when she saw the wedding ring. He laughed quietly to himself as he started up the church steps. After all, she'd said she wanted a band. *A present for the bride and a second chance for the groom,* he thought in spite of himself.

"Okay, Johnnie," Matt said. "Let's get it done."

Perri walked back through the front door of Gledhill a married woman. She crossed the threshold alone. The groom had let her out at the door before garaging his car with nary a word.

Neither bride nor groom had had much to say since the brief reception at the Ransoms'. The whole thing had left Perri subdued and silent. After all, never before had she set foot on Ransom land. Never, until her wedding day. Scandal and barbed wire had always separated her from Matt's world.

As Perri slowly climbed the stairs, her wedding ring caught her eye. Invisibly set, princess-cut diamonds accented the pearshaped emerald. A band. She had selected a plain, gold band. Obviously, this wasn't the wedding ring *she'd* picked out.

"No, it's the one *I* picked out," he had said with a devilish grin.

Damn his hide. It was stunning. It matched the emerald and diamond earrings he had given her the night before. In the hot tub. It had taken everything she had not to slide facedown into the turbulent water after that kiss. Of course she had worn the earrings for the wedding.

"The emeralds match the green lights in your eyes, if I'm not mistaken." Matt had studied her in the softly glowing light of the spare little church. "You look beautiful, even more beautiful than usual, Mrs. Ransom," he'd added.

And now, he had let her cross the threshold alone in order to park his car. She could just spit. Perri closed the door to her bedroom and began to undress. This was as rough on Matt as it was on her, she reminded herself. She recalled the fury with which he had lashed out at her that night twelve years before. He'd clearly stated then that he wouldn't shame his family by marrying the daughter of a Marlowe woman.

And yet, now they were married. Now, they had a second chance. Or, maybe she was just being pathetically hopeful. This was, after all, an arranged marriage. Her thoughts scattered at the perfunctory knock. The door opened, abruptly returning her to the present.

Well, unwrap this, he thought in shock. "That's what you were wearing to get married in a church?" he demanded, moving toward her. "What are you trying to do? Kill me?"

"Next time knock, and then wait for permission, will you?"

she sputtered. Perri had been so lost in her own thoughts, his footsteps on the stairs hadn't registered.

"Flowers for the bride," he said unwrapping a box of long-stemmed pink roses and selecting one still drawn into a bud. Matt slowly started toward her.

Annoyed, flustered and three-quarters naked, she stood before him in thigh-high, lace-topped stockings, an ivory silk bra and matching thong. She clutched at her dress as he took his time looking her over. "It was too hot for a lot of underwear, okay?" she declared weakly. The look in his eyes only made her weaker.

"Okay," he replied as the rose drew a soft line down her arm. Her dress somehow melted out of her hands. He slowly stroked her bare stomach, studying her. He watched her nipples tighten, mirroring the pink bud he held to her throat.

Matt seemed intent on murdering her with tenderness, while memorizing every line and curve. Perri quivered at the gentle touch. It was all those hot, stolen moments together in the past that now led to such lazy sweetness. His tongue moved gradually past her lips as he carefully drew her into his arms. His big hands heated her flesh and her blood. Suddenly dropping the rose, Matt pulled her hips against his rigid flesh.

She went pliant in his arms as his hand slid down to grip her thong, twisting the tiny scrap of material around his knuckles and pulling it taut. He held her tethered by the silk as he lightly bit her lips. All the while, Matt kept pulling so the thong rasped gently into her tender folds.

Startled, Perri gasped at the sensation. It was almost too much. The moment had rapidly shifted from sweet to hot, with Matt in command. She melted as his hungry lips moved to her throat. He was getting too close.

Perri couldn't let him see how vulnerable she felt. If he got too close, she knew Matt would realize that she still loved him. She loved him and her heart ached for it. She couldn't keep it sex instead of intimacy. She froze in his arms at the sudden understanding that it just wasn't possible for her. He couldn't help but feel her sudden alarm.

Nothing else would have ended the moment more successfully. Matt knew her well; he'd pushed too hard. He reined in on the desire that all but consumed him. She had every right to expect him to take it slower than this.

"I have to see to the stock. One of the mares has a strain," he said, squeezing the globes of her bottom. "We may be in for some weather by tonight. Don't wait dinner for me," he added. "I'll be back when I get back." For a moment he held her as if he had something more to say. Then, patting her hip, he moved toward the door.

"Thank you for the roses, Matt," Perri called softly after him. She took a deep breath as he closed the door, willing her heated blood to cool.

She heard Matt walk toward the bedroom he had claimed for himself. What a useful skill running was, Perri realized with some bitterness. You were moving forward, so you didn't have to look at how you were really moving away. Your focus was forward. You were taking an action that at least had the pretense of being positive.

The kinesthetic approach, and the effort of running, took your mind off what you were moving away from. "Yeah, run along, Matt," she whispered in the empty room. She was trembling.

Second chances weren't the only things you could avoid thinking about when you were running, Perri reminded herself. Not if you had something important enough to do.

She dragged a hand through her hair. Where had all the anguish and regret come from? She took the time now to really examine the question. How much of it was because twelve years ago she had dragged her heart to Raleigh and kept going? The past was still there between them; a past engineered by Leila Ransom. There was no getting around it.

The door slammed open.

"How come you never got married?" Matt demanded. He had tried to leave it alone, to be a gentleman about it. Too bad. He was working hard to build something here, even though the memory of past events seemed to always shimmer on the edge of his vision. He had had to get away from her to pull himself together. Once when he'd parked the car, and now in order to change for his work.

Neither one of them seemed at all skilled in bridging this gap.

He noticed that Perri hadn't moved during the time it had taken him to change into his work clothes. She seemed frozen and bewildered by the question. Too bad.

"This marriage should have been mine for life, Mrs. Ransom," he stated flatly, his eyes unreadable. When she didn't reply he went on. "You'll answer the question someday soon. You will give me that much before you're on your way out of here," he added.

Matt turned away in disgust. Disgust at himself. At life and its consequences. And most especially, at his own blundering pride and his all-consuming hunger for a woman he shouldn't want.

He's turned away again, she thought. *On his way out the door.* That did it. Fueled from its differing points of origin, Perri's anger raged like fire on a prairie wind. Her fury over the events of twelve years ago finally joined with her distress over the fact that she still cared for him after all this time. Now it burst into white-hot flames in the present moment.

She threw her wedding dress at his retreating back. The edge she felt was vicious. "Listen up, Ransom, and listen good," she demanded. "I'm not going anywhere. I'm staying!" Perri remained rooted to one spot, as if proving her point. "And you're going to need to deal with that. So you can stop telling me what I'm going to do," she said in cold fury.

"I let myself be pushed away without a fight once before, but that doesn't mean you call all the shots," she said furiously. "It doesn't mean you can haul me back now just because you feel like it. Now that you need me for something other than sex," she added.

Matt stood silently with his despair. She had never looked more beautiful. "And I'll have what I need from you the minute the six months are up, won't I?" he said bleakly. It wasn't really a question.

Some wedding day, Perri thought as she listened, yet again, to his boots on the stairs.

Matt moved through the darkness toward Gledhill's back porch, his pickup parked on Ransom land. Even when he reached the back door, he didn't know what he was going to say to her. He understood Perri well enough to think she might still be in love with him; some at least. He prayed she loved him enough to get them through this emotional storm.

He was furious that he couldn't just take what was so obviously his, due to his pride. And the past. To be matter-of-fact about it, he just didn't see how he could live with Perri and not have her. He had no hope for a marriage in name only. Not when she looked at him the way she did. Not when he knew how she heated every time he got his hands on her. He passed silently through the kitchen.

Just out of the shower, and no calmer for her efforts, Perri heard the now-familiar sound of boots on the stairs. "Matt." The way she said it sounded like an oath. Racing into her room from the connecting bath, she barely had time to throw on a pair of silk pajama bottoms and work herself into her bra. She heard him move down the hall toward her bedroom as she grabbed for her pajama top. She didn't attempt to button it. The knob was already turning.

He opened the door and halted, considering her. His eyes raked over her, then rested on her tightening nipples. His lazy, perfunctory knock after the fact signaled that the niceties were not going to be observed.

From the look of him, he had showered and changed clothes at Ransoms'. Whether he expected dinner or not she really couldn't say. He certainly hadn't called to let her know his plans. Perri took a deep breath. "Don't you ever honor a closed door, Matt?" she demanded furiously.

"No," he said as he started slowly forward, considering her. "Not when my bride is behind it. Not on my wedding night. Not," he whispered as he stopped in front of her, "when it's you."

Matt didn't stop to think. He took her in his arms before she could make up her mind whether or not to back off. His hands moved hungrily under her shirt, over the bare skin of her back as his kiss broke down her defenses. As he'd hoped, her anger transformed into hot, urgent desire. They had both seen this moment coming.

"If you're going to say no, say it now," he demanded.

She couldn't.

He knew it. He played with her mouth for what seemed like forever. Teasing, openmouthed kisses left her breathless as he removed her pajama top and fancy bra in a heartbeat.

Matt sucked in a breath as he noted the changes womanhood had brought about to her breasts. She was still small and beautifully formed. But she had ripened. His fingers reverently brushed the undersides of each plump little globe. He took his time to thoroughly explore her. She was damp from her shower and the scent of soap clung to her curves. Perri swayed into him with a moan.

The silk charmeuse bra had led him to assume she was wearing matching panties. His desire jolted up a level when his hands covered her bottom. She was wearing nothing underneath those soft, silky pants.

She felt his surprise as work-roughened fingers snagged on the delicate silk. "You didn't give me time," she explained as her arms circled his waist. She kissed him as she pulled determinedly at his T-shirt. After working it over his head, her hungry mouth moved down to that gorgeous chest. Perri took in the scent of his skin as her tongue found his nipple.

Matt returned the favor. He pulled her head back and let his mouth tantalize her breasts. His hand roamed down over her hips. He played with her navel, tickling and lightly slapping her with the ends of the drawstring holding up the pajamas that rode low on her hips. He then untied the little bow and slowly stripped her. Grabbing her shoulders, Matt abruptly turned her to the wall.

Hitting the switch for the overhead light, he carefully braced her facing the wall of the darkened room. The light from the bath and the hall played over each side of her back and hips.

Slowly, Matt filled his hands with her on a hoarse groan. The tension between them intensified. Her back burned as his chest pressed against her. Perri arched into him when the stubble of his beard rasped against the nape of her neck.

Perri couldn't stop the roll of her hips that brought her into contact with jeans pulled tight over his raised flesh. His thumbs toyed with her erect nipples, before he gently raked a thumbnail over each. She rolled her hips even harder and gasped at his touch.

"You always did respond to that," he said as he lightly pinched each heated crest. "I remember every little detail of you." His teeth gently tugged on her earlobe. "Since you've been back, you're all I can think about, all I can smell. I can already taste you again, darlin'," he said in a low, urgent voice.

Whatever combination of desire and caring he had fantasized about finding again with Perri, the reality of now made those fantasies pale. She threw him so off balance with her honesty and generous nature. She had been big-eyed, long-legged and coltish as a teenager. Now, a woman moved erotically under his hands.

She trembled as those hands boldly journeyed down and around the globes of her bottom. Fingers lightly drummed on her flesh, at her hips, around the protruding bones; up and down the outside of her thighs. Then again over her buttocks. She yielded to the wall in what seemed a caress. She could no longer support herself on her arms.

"Open your legs for me," he demanded in a whisper. Determined fingers made their way toward the inside of her thighs from the back. Perri complied.

Matt had a notion of playing with her until she whimpered. She was whimpering now, her hips slowly grinding against him in a rhythmic appeal. He had intended to make her wait. He hadn't intended to find himself so close to the border where his own reason completely dissolved.

He pulled her against him, away from the wall and held her with one arm. Her breasts rested on his forearm and his erection cradled against her buttocks. Perri moaned as his hand found its way over her belly, between her sensitive inner thighs, into the presence of her heat.

He could feel that enticing warmth just out of his reach. He tortured himself with restraint, then moved his fingers to slowly drum against her moist folds. When Matt slowly ground his hips against her buttocks, Perri didn't melt. She ignited. His touch became more determined, less playful. Her climax was swift and hard. The way she cried out his name ripped into him.

He quickly turned her around to face him, and the electric jolt of his naked chest against her breasts almost buckled his knees. His mouth assaulted hers. Judgment had fled, as he picked her up and moved quickly to the bed.

Matt jerked back the covers and settled Perri down. She watched his boots hit the floor and the accompanying swift struggle with his jeans. She knew as he followed her onto the bed, nudging his way between her legs and filling her eager mouth with his tongue, her body knew. There was no room for thought. It was Matt her body responded to so freely, yet it was a man's body she now cradled. A man's strength, a man's hands, mouth and hunger taking possession. This was not the young Matt who had first claimed her for his own.

Matt tore himself free of the kiss to look at her. Then with slow deliberation, he kissed his way down her body as it glowed in the low light. His mouth was so gentle, the slight stubble of his beard only tickled her. Matt's underlying power remained fully mastered and contained. The careful approach, coupled with his awareness of his own strength made her melt all over again with desire. Her back slowly arched as his tongue searched out the little bud of nerves concealed within her damp curls. She writhed against the gentle lashing and tried desperately to bring him ever closer.

Perri gave out with a protesting moan when he finally pulled back to look at her. Matt smiled at the sound. She looked breathtaking, wanton. She'd always been beautiful to him. And he had let her go.

His hand slowly and heavily followed the same path his lips had taken from her throat, over her aroused breasts. She moaned again when he paused to roll her nipple between his fingers before his hand continued its journey down between her thighs. A world of memory and regret resided in the heavy stroke.

His fingers rested gently against her sleek folds. Matt stopped there, watching her in the low light. Perri gasped and deliberately moved against his hand. She was so hot and so very wet. The feel of how much she wanted him, how ready she was for his entry made him grit his teeth.

"Matt," she pleaded, reaching for him.

He leaned forward to kiss her breast, taking her deeply into his mouth, as he eased his fingers deep inside her damp sheath. He moved his lips to her mouth, his tongue taking possession, as they both reveled in the well-remembered sensation of his flesh on hers. He had meant his kisses to soothe them both, but the scent that was so uniquely hers finally undid the last of his restraint.

Hoping to slow himself down, he pulled back to his knees. Matt took a deep, hissing breath when he felt a soft, slender hand close around him. His hips pumped involuntarily before he could pull her hand away and drape her legs over his arms. He paused to look at her. His gaze moved from the damp folds that called him to join his body with hers up to her eyes.

Perri found the sensation of being so open and vulnerable to this man highly erotic. "Please, Matt," she whispered, "now."

Well, that did it. The weight of the years that had kept them apart vanished as he slowly entered her. She was so hot and so very wet. She smiled when they began to move together in a rhythm as old as the earth; as easy with each other as if it were yesterday when they had last joined. Holding her legs, he watched the effect his body had on hers. He wanted to see her eyes as he moved within her.

Matt shook under the effort it took to keep from cutting loose. He wanted her with him. He finally broke his hold on her legs and rested his weight onto his arms. She immediately wrapped her legs around him, holding him close. "Look at me," he demanded through clenched teeth. She immediately complied.

The sight of him, his body slick with sweat and so fierce, took her breath away. He made her frantic to give him anything he wanted. He looked so dazzling above her as he thrust into her. There wasn't a wasted move between them.

Perri assumed she would regret this night. She chose to accept any regrets with the certainty of how much more she would regret this night never happening. The heat burst within them as they both caught fire in a sudden, hot rush toward fulfillment.

Matt cried out her name as he felt tiny, feminine muscles ripple around him. He collapsed onto her, burying his face at the base of her neck; his short supply of tears falling undetected into the thick, velvety mass of her hair.

The night wind was picking up; he could hear it swirling through the trees out back. To Matt, the long, lonesome sound was both soothing and familiar. He automatically offered up a silent prayer for rain, while he felt himself restored to the present. As the old house adjusted to the return of the night wind, it occurred to him that what he had missed for years had now been restored.

Making love to other women, having sex, had always been every possible combination of tender, funny, affectionate, hot or raunchy. But with no one else had he experienced anything like this. With Perri, he felt himself depart from his own separate spirit to join on a deeper level than the physical. With Perri, it was somehow more intimate. He sighed contentedly and lay still, listening to the house and the wind. And then, he heard the "click."

Matt frowned, puzzled. It had almost sounded to him as if someone had thrown the light switch, pitching the room into darkness. But nothing had changed. Light still spilled over them from the hallway and the adjoining bathroom. He had hit the switch himself shortly after entering her room.

Suddenly, he understood. It was Perri. The sound hadn't been audible. But it had come from her, from that deeper level. She had departed from him. All of that vibrant passion had withdrawn, vanished as if it had never been. *Dammit,* he thought sadly. They were still joined and she'd managed to run from him. He wasn't having it.

Matt raised up onto his arms and looked at her, ready to bring her back to him any way he could. But instead, she took his breath away.

Her lips were swollen and red, her eyes so dilated, they almost matched his own for darkness. It wasn't the face of a starry-eyed girl, safe in the arms of her first love. It was the face of a woman who, try as she might to fight it, was bound to him on that deeper level.

He grinned at her as something deep inside him relaxed. "You regret it already, don't you?'' Matt nipped at her chin in a manner a little too slow and knowing to be considered playful.

"This doesn't settle anything, Ransom," she declared, trying to avoid the caress. Tiny, internal muscles squeezed involuntarily around him.

He laughed softly when she couldn't quite refrain from arching into him. His teeth tugged on her earlobe. "I don't know, hon," he answered. "I feel fairly well settled in some very significant ways, myself." His mouth moved to her already budding nipple and beyond. As Matt slid down her body to place openmouthed kisses on the undersides of her breasts, the stubble of his beard rasped her skin just enough to bring pleasure.

Did her body have to betray her right now? Perri restlessly adjusted her legs. She had a point to make, if she could just keep in mind what it was. If he would cut it out, she could think of how to phrase what she had to say.

"Maybe you're right," Perri announced reasonably. "Maybe this does settle something. Now that we've gotten the sex out of the way, maybe we can manage to talk to each other. To work together," she added. The thought brightened her mood. "Now maybe we can talk some things through."

Matt's response to such statements was to draw her breast deeply into his mouth, in a caress that would have been too rough before. "Out of the way?" he asked as he continued to tease and nuzzle her tender skin. "I do appreciate the way your breasts have grown up, darlin'." His tongue lightly skipped over her nipple.

As Perri gasped, Matt moved back up and cradled her jaw in his broad hands. "But that just took the edge off," he declared. "Honey, I haven't had nearly enough of you for you to be thinking that the sex is 'out of the way.' And——" he grinned "——you haven't had nearly enough of me."

His tongue swept the automatic and immediate protest from her mouth. Perri could feel herself losing all reason. He didn't demand. He didn't have to. Matt naturally commanded a response from her. She was getting intoxicated just on the taste of him. It felt as if her bones were melting; as if he could mold her into anything he wanted.

How could there be even more wild heat between them? She just didn't get it. Perri had felt sanity return only moments ago. She had even managed to achieve some distance; distance that had given her a precious and necessary grip on her heart.

Then, all he had to do was take one little love bite and she'd melted all over again. Her hips ground wantonly in a move impossible to stop. "You insufferable, egotistical jerk," she said, glaring at him when his mouth finally released hers.

He didn't take offense. Didn't bother to deny it. "Yeah, but I'm your insufferable, egotistical jerk."

"Are you, Matt?"

That put a momentary halt on him. Matt humbly searched her face for a long time before he spoke. "I'm your husband," he reminded her. "Do you really want to talk about anything else right now?"

She was abruptly aware of just how heavy and full he'd become. Just as abruptly, all the fight went out of her, as the desire between them compounded with each successive moment. She paused, considering him just as he was considering her.

The light played over his face, highlighting the hard angles just enough for her to see an unexpected appeal in his dark eyes. "No," Perri stated without artifice, as she moved to wrap her legs around his waist. "No, I don't."

"Such a sad face," he said tenderly. "Well, if you're so determined to regret this night, then I'd better give you something to regret. Don't you think, hon?" Matt kissed her urgently as his mood switched away from the tenderness of the moment before.

He was determined to maintain that deeper connection with her and build on it. Determined to build a new life for both of them. If it took him awhile to get her to stay with him in that deeper region, well, they had all night, he reasoned. He had no intention of wasting a moment of it.

"I'd better see to it you've got something worth regretting, then," he said again. In one quick move, he drove himself into her. "Do you regret this, Perri?" he asked, moving inside her. Forcefully. "Or this? Or this?"

Each thrust brought her back to him, until she was ready to splinter and reform on that deeper level. There were no defenses she could build or maintain against him. He wasn't rough with her, he was purposeful. "Do you regret how I can make you feel, Perri?" His intention was clear. "Tell me!" he commanded. "Do I feel like something you should regret?" Rough palms cupped her bottom and held her even more tightly to him.

On a low, reckless moan, Perri's nails scored down his back. She pulled him even deeper into her in a silent demand. Taking him as he was taking her. Her mouth went in search of his. Her tongue probed delicately at first, and then with red-hot determination. She wanted all of him and she wanted him now. The demand was as plainly stated as if it had been voiced. He had managed to reach her on a level too deep for anything less than honesty.

Matt broke the kiss, smiling over her little moan of protest. "You're close to desperate for me to finish it, aren't you?" he asked. "Aren't you?" He watched her eyes glaze as she tightened around him. "Do you regret that, Perri? I'll just bet you do. Would you regret my loving you?" he whispered.

The last query was voiced so softly, she wasn't certain it was real. Each stroke went deeper within her than she would have thought possible. He was touching her in a way that was far more intimate than the physical. Matt kept consuming her, steady and strong, long after she caught fire beneath him.

The drive to Spirit Lake occurred in silence. Matt hadn't looked at her since they'd climbed into the pickup. When he'd started the engine, the radio had played Mary Chapin Carpenter singing "Hometown Girl." Matt had quickly turned it off. This was hard enough.

Just driving out to the lake brought back too many memories. Perri reminded herself that there was no point now in feeling any embarrassment for some of the things she had let him do in his pickup. She would have let him do anything he'd wanted. She had loved him so much. Nor was there any sense to this awkwardness she felt over their wedding night. It had happened.

Matt turned off and parked in the shade of a tree on Gannie's land. Saying nothing, he scooted out from under the wheel. He gently stroked her cheek with the back of his fingers, before drawing her soft weight against him. Taking her hand, he played lightly with her palm.

Matt carefully but inexorably pulled her a little closer to him. He hadn't let her retreat completely after that night. Heartbeats in unison, they watched the skiers for a time, each with their own private thoughts.

Before now, she had never reflected much upon the obligation of an inheritance. Even when Gannie had mentioned some vague details about leaving Perri and Matt the responsibility of the project, Perri hadn't really understood. If Gannie hadn't exacted such conditions concerning the estate, what would she have done? *Be miserable*, Perri thought. *I'd probably feel obliged to sell and it would kill me.*

"Come on," Matt said, opening the door to the pickup and helping her out. For a time they just wandered over the property, with no clue as to what Gannie might have had in mind.

It was nothing special. Nor was it a sorry piece of land. The property sat above Spirit Lake doing nothing interesting; doing nothing to inspire a brainstorm regarding its use.

Finally Matt spoke. "No matter what happens, Perri," he said. "No matter how it all turns out, I'm your partner in this. I can take care of the land. I can protect and add to the property. And I can take care of and protect you. I will provide for you," he vowed solemnly, "and I won't mistreat you."

If I could still love you, I would, he thought, turning his gaze toward the deep-blue water. His six months with Perri might be all the living instead of being deadened he'd ever have. Matt just didn't have the energy, the "need to fight" in order to regain the power to feel.

But he felt the need to pledge his support to Perri; to make some sort of promise that might lay a foundation for trust. It was the best he could do to further his own redemption.

"Thank you for that. I want it to matter, Matt," she said as she walked into his open arms. "I want what we do here to matter, at least a little."

I want it to matter, even if I don't, Perri reflected as she turned her head to watch the skiers. Even if their marriage didn't matter to him like it did to her. Even if she didn't really matter to Matt, something Perri did, some action she took, would matter. If only to Gannie.

"Let's go home, Matt," she said as he hugged her to him. "Thank you for pledging to take care of me." It meant something.

He ached for her. He wanted to say more. And yet the bottom fell out every time he tried to take the next step. He just didn't have it in him.

No, maybe that wasn't honest. He may have had it in him. But Matt Ransom had no way left to seize what might still be there. In order to rebuild that charred and ruined bridge, he reckoned he'd need heart. And he just didn't have the heart.

"Okay, we'll go home," Matt said cupping her chin in his hand. "I want you, hon. I need you. Feel like moving into my room tonight?" he inquired lightly. "If not, I seem to recall that once upon a time you were rather partial to my pickup."

They smiled at each other. A woman who couldn't stop loving and running; and a man who hadn't learned that standing still froze his feelings.

"Not yet, Matt," Perri said, blushing. "I need just a little more time."

Matt paused to hold her before helping her into the cab of the pickup.

An understanding, sensitive Matt Ransom. It's almost too good to be true, Perri thought as he kissed her and started for home. Later she would see the whole thing as just part of his strategy to get her to live with him without so much fuss.

Nausea. Nausea had never claimed her whole body before. Nausea had never caused all of her senses to hum like this. This was different. It had never before affected her hearing or her vision, flooding her until she felt light-headed.

What was going on? Why this sudden fatigue? *The fatigue must be why I'm so nauseous,* she reasoned. Perri pulled the car over by the bridge across the tracks and brought both hands to her clammy cheeks. Her swollen breasts stung. She was so tired.

No, Perri thought firmly. She dismissed the idea that reluctantly formed as impossible. *It's too early to really know.*

She would get herself home and into bed just as soon as she stopped shaking long enough to drive the car. What were the early warning signs anyway? Oh, Lord, she would have to call some girlfriends in New York for that.

She was grateful they were now sleeping in separate bedrooms, and had been for almost a month. Matt had gotten too close on their wedding night. Too close to her. Loving him as she did, Perri had requested a period of adjustment.

She had needed time to sort things out. She had given him so much of herself once before; and had been so violently rent apart. It had become easier to forgive herself for surrendering so totally to him at seventeen. She was older, wiser, more mature; and still she couldn't have stopped him if she'd tried.

But still, her wariness and embarrassment over how he could control her sexually, and his shameless use of that advantage, had formed an apex where the different paths of her anguish came together. She was stupid with him, she acknowledged to herself bitterly as she rested her clammy forehead on the steering wheel. In a stupor every time he touched her. Being pulled to him only to be pushed away was undignified, even if he was struggling himself.

Now she had even more on her shoulders. Maybe with separate bedrooms and baths, she could keep him from finding out every time she felt sick like this. When she felt better, she vowed to drive to a drugstore for a home test. Maybe drive to the next county for it. She had to think this through before Matt's feelings about this little life just beginning inside her colored her own joy. *At least I'll have his child,* she thought, *no matter what happens.*

Taking a deep breath to steady herself, she signaled before she pulled back out onto Route 66.

Four

Lightning woke him before the thunder could. For a moment he lay in the darkness of the second-story bedroom, taking in the music and feel of a storm over Gledhill. Matt felt surrounded by weather, rather than burrowed down into Ransom land.

It was an interesting sensation on the hill, he noted. To feel suspended rather than grounded. As was his custom, he counted off the time between lightning and thunder. It would be right on top of them within minutes. A good night to learn how the old house took to a storm.

Well, it would do. The house had courage, he determined. *Courage out in the open,* Matt thought, as he toured the ground floor. *Just like Gannie.* She was with him as he moved out onto the glass-enclosed back porch to watch the show.

The lightning strikes were moving rapidly overhead. *I'll bet it's over 200 per second,* he reflected, consulting his internal clock. How Gannie must have loved to watch the night from here. He loved it as well. Unlike Perri, wild weather made him feel alive. Always had.

Perri. Without thinking about it, Matt turned and headed for the stairs. She had always been fearful of the noise, the potential for violence. Once before, she had trembled and clung to him; first out of fear, and then out of desire, as thunder and lightning had pierced the tranquillity of Gledhill.

Matt moved swiftly to her door, and stood watching her sleep. *Good,* he thought with relief, *she needs it.* Perri had been driving herself with such intensity for the last month, she was worn down to where you could almost see the steel.

He moved quietly into the room. She looked peaceful now. And so beautiful he ached just to hold her. *My wife,* he thought as he sat beside her on the bed. It meant something so different from what he had always assumed it would.

She slept on through the thunder and Matt breathed easier for it. If the woman could sleep through this, she was stronger, more centered and more secure than the girl she had been. He smiled as he gently touched a lock of her hair. Her scent reached him, bringing him comfort. It eased the ever-present desire he felt for the woman sleeping alone.

She was probably going to have a fit when she learned of his plans, he figured, playing with the curls. But maybe he had been right to rapidly institute as many changes as possible. Maybe if he could put the past aside, initiate an assault on it, somehow he could forgive and forget.

And then maybe he could let go. Let go of the burden of knowing he had caused Perri to leave town. Of knowing that his breaking up with her and so quickly getting engaged to Cadie had driven Perri to have an abortion in Raleigh. Ever since his mother had told him that Perri had called from Raleigh with the news, there had been no going back. It still hurt that Perri hadn't even asked to speak with him at the time. *His baby.* Matt didn't dwell on how he had felt about that, not anymore. Not after Cadie's misfortune. It was past.

Every day now he debated whether or not to give back the locket Perri had returned when she'd left town. *Would it help heal wounds or rub them too raw for them to talk things through?* he wondered. She should know that he considered himself the one responsible. She should know he understood what she must have gone through at seventeen. Alone.

Action never won out in these internal debates, Matt realized as he started for the hall. He didn't know how to talk things out. It didn't come naturally. It just hadn't been done and he didn't have a lot of hope in his skills.

Matt turned in the darkness, for better or worse alone in the storm. He watched his new wife sleep peacefully as lightning continued to strike without any regard for the inhabitants on the hill.

Perri and Donnie silently took in the chaos which, at the moment, centered around Matt and John in Gannie's former bedroom. "How many 800 numbers did you call?" Perri inquired dryly.

"A few," Matt responded as he tightened a bolt on the biggest, shiniest brass bed he had been able to find.

Matt and John, both shirtless in the air-conditioning, had gotten the room down to ground zero and beyond. Brand-new bookshelves and new chests of drawers were already in place.

Perri decided it was a fortunate thing that the master bedroom was so big. That bed was ridiculous. It was embarrassing. And she couldn't help but notice that the man had positioned it to take advantage of the full-length mirror. She could just imagine why. "You're going to need to wear sunglasses to get any sleep," Perri said sweetly.

Matt's look let her know the plan here didn't include getting a lot of sleep. "From what I can tell," he answered just as sweetly, "you can sleep through just about anything."

"I still can't believe you didn't wake me!" Three hundred lightning strikes-per-second over Spirit, and he had let her sleep through it. "I'm horrified, not to mention feeling cheated," Perri added.

"Well, it didn't seem like that much at the time," Donnie said to no one in particular, "especially since we never got any rain."

"Well, of course it didn't seem like much at the time," John chimed in. "The state got over 20,000 strikes within a six-hour period. What's a few hundred-per-second over this place?"

"Don't worry, Mrs. Ransom, I'll make absolutely certain you're awake next time around," Matt said with a lazy grin, "even if it is three a.m." He sighed nobly. "I'll find some way to keep you awake."

Perri couldn't help the blush. Her breathing shortened and her body began to tingle at his look. She'd seen this coming. He'd been sensitive and respectful of her need to remain apart for the last month and to take things slowly. But he had been as nice and as understanding as he was going to get. Patience had never been Matt Ransom's strong suit. And who was she kidding? She wanted him.

She would be sharing this room with him before they were many days older. The look he was giving her made that clear. It blazed as much as the summer heat pulsing on the other side of the window. And he was not unaware of how her body felt about it, either.

Matt continued to grin at her, enjoying the flush of color on her face. He couldn't wait to see Perri in the middle of his bed. Messy, rumpled and well-loved. He'd wanted a new bed for them, one he'd never slept in with anyone else. One that was theirs; one with no history.

There's too damn much of the past in this house, he thought sternly. He was hell-bent on getting Perri out of the past when she looked at her surroundings. When she looked at him. When he looked at her.

"Why don't you two go down and figure out what to do with the dining room," John suggested. "We cleared a wall. The photographs of the pioneer women, and the tapes and transcripts of the 89ers are stored down there along with the computer equipment. Decide where you want what."

"The past with the present," Donnie stated, grinning at him. "Gannie would have liked that."

"What?" he demanded. Whenever LaDonna Marlowe grinned like that, John automatically got suspicious.

"You," she answered. "Out of your suit. Somehow you always look more real to me in a pair of old jeans. Not that you don't wear those fancy suits well," Donnie added quickly. "I was thinking about that at the funeral. Gannie sure arranged some fine-looking pallbearers for herself," she remarked as she strolled toward the hall.

John shook his head in mock sorrow. "I thought they raised you better than that," he said.

"They raised her well enough to see about feeding you," Perri laughed. "We'll holler when it's ready."

On the descent down the stairs, Perri couldn't help but notice how different this place was from Matt's home. During the reception, she had shamelessly inspected the Ransom place. The old house had given her the impression that it could be cleaned and straightened in record time. The furnishings were masculine and simple. There was nothing fussy. Nothing that communicated any reminders of a genteel heritage left back in the East. Everything seemed to point to a family born right here. Born for Oklahoma, and intending to stay.

The western style, built from the ground up for the comfort of large men who favored saddle leather and wood, suited both the Ransoms and the family business. The house was such a contrast to Gledhill. It was so flat. Hidden from the road, the big, sprawling one-story structure literally nestled down among the elms and hugged the earth. She had wondered how many generations had added onto the original building.

Oddly enough, it was also a home shorn of all feminine touches. While it seemed a little out of balance, it also seemed right. It brought relief, as if a certain amount of strain or effort had been deleted from the atmosphere. Perri had found herself grateful not to be staring at some terribly grand portrait of Leila hanging on a wall in a place of honor, or one of Matt's Grandma Ransom.

Up on the hill, Gledhill had been built by a Yankee, determined to assert his position in the community. With its cathedral ceiling over most of the house, it looked poised as if to one day take to the air. The fact that it never had was a testament to how well built it had been. It wasn't the best type of dwelling for Tornado Alley; anyone could see that. But it did make a statement.

The Ransom place, however, had been built for Miss Vienna by plainsmen. It fit perfectly with the land. Everything Perri had heard about the place had come flooding back. Miss Vienna Whitaker had bought the homestead of a farmer who couldn't maintain his claim after a vicious winter. It was a common enough story for the time.

Although in this instance, the story was spiced with rumors that Miss Vienna had used what was to have been her dowry to pay for the place. She had, forthwith, set about replacing the sod dwelling with a genuine house.

Perri had been immediately drawn to inspect the original, handmade shutters as soon as she'd entered for the reception. She and Donnie had always heard about those shutters. Each had a series of rifle slots in the thick wood that opened and closed as necessary. The Ransoms were bunkered down in defense of more than Mother Nature's supernatural winds.

At Sam's insistence, Matt had given her a brief tour of the stables. The sight of the colts with the mares was the instant when Perri gave her heart to big, soft eyes, long eyelashes and to muzzles that felt like velvet.

A little sorrel colt was losing his baby coat. Perri had always wondered at the difference in a sorrel and a roan. Now she could see it. He would be all roan soon. She had never thought about colts doing that—losing their baby hair. It was so sweet. Everywhere she'd looked, she had fallen in love. In love with Matt Ransom's world.

Perri now realized that just as the Ransom place was bereft of any feminine touches, Gledhill was without any masculine presence—except for what Perri had captured in the memory box a lifetime ago. *Fancy work everywhere you look,* she thought.

She followed as Donnie pushed her way through the kitchen's swinging doors. The kitchen was indisputably the heart of the old house.

"I don't suppose we could just set out some fruit and cottage cheese," Donnie remarked.

"If you set the table, I'll see about some chicken and salad," Perri answered, moving to the refrigerator. They worked quickly, with the ease of women in a familiar kitchen.

She got the chicken to warming and looked around. The kitchen, the breakfast nook and the back porch were the only downstairs rooms that didn't resemble a museum. The longer she contemplated her surroundings, the stronger her conviction became that using the land Gannie had donated to Spirit as the site for yet another museum was not the answer.

Suddenly, the smell of chicken assaulted her senses and Perri bustled out into the dining room for some much-needed air. Donnie quickly followed.

"Have you told him?" Donnie asked quietly, placing a cold, damp towel to Perri's throat.

"No," she replied weakly. "Is it obvious?"

"Well, if I just figured it out—"

"Donnie, I can't," Perri said. "Not yet. I don't know how." Nausea kept throwing her off her stride these days. Lately, she had been so tightly wound she could almost twitch.

Donnie put her arms around her cousin. "I'm so sorry, hon," she said. "Sorry for the situation, not sorry for a baby. But to see you like this just breaks my heart."

Perri hugged her back. "I didn't think anything else would ever hurt me as deeply again. Leila hurt. Leaving hurt. Finding out Matt was getting married six weeks after I left town, to some girl from Sapulpa, hurt even worse," she said, pressing the towel to her forehead. "His wife pregnant, so soon after their marriage just about killed me. Things happened too fast. Now they're happening too fast again. I can't take another hurt, Donnie. I don't think I have it in me."

"Have you ever said anything to Matt about Leila threatening you into leaving?" Donnie asked. She leaned against the bachelor's table. "Did you say anything that night?"

"No. And we haven't talked about it since that night. I just don't know how to say it," Perri replied sadly. "We haven't spoken about what happened since I was seventeen years old. And I was in such shock at seeing my whole world crumble, I couldn't think straight enough to say anything in my own defense. But it's not going to help much to bring it up now if the timing isn't right."

"Talk to him, Per," Donnie urged. "Tell Matt what happened. All of it. He has a right to know."

"Why would he want to hear about the past?" Perri asked wearily. "He's been hammering on me to let it go as it is. Why would he even listen to anything I'd say about his mother? But of course, I'll tell him about the baby. Directly.''

"It's time," Donnie replied firmly. "Now that there's a child to consider. Now is the time for you to stop running from it, now that Leila is dead. You would never have survived as her daughter-in-law, under her roof," she added. "You may not realize it even now, but when you left for Raleigh, you were running for your life."

"But this is so humiliating," Perri blurted out. "To have a man forced, first into marrying me and now into fatherhood. He's been forced into a superficial relationship in order to inherit something that should be his unconditionally."

She turned and stared at the wall against which Gannie's tapes and transcripts of the Land Run were now being stored. As a distraction, it was a beaut. Perri and Donnie had a lot of work to do; for a lot of work had gone into the project. Gannie had started right out of college collecting the individual histories of the 89ers who had still been alive at the time. Propped against the wall alongside the tapes and transcripts were a series of photographs of sculptures of pioneer women. Gannie had set great store in her photographs of the final entries from which the Pioneer Woman Monument at Ponca City had been chosen.

If the kitchen was the heart of the old house, the photographs of the Pioneer Women sculptures were its soul. Now heart and soul resided side by side.

Gannie had said those photographs reminded her never to quit. To continue to search for the stories of women who had played out their lives in an effort to build a home and a life on the red earth. Women who, in many instances, had had no vote and no voice in the decision to come West. Women who, often as not, were buried alongside the rivers and creeks in nameless graves.

The sculptures had always fascinated Perri and Donnie. Some were obviously too sensuous to have been chosen for the monument at Ponca; some too rigid or unfeeling.

"My favorite is going right here." Donnie pointed to a prominent spot, dead center. "I'll go get the hammer."

Perri smiled after her. Donnie's favorite entry was a striking sculpture of a Native American woman, bareheaded and nursing a baby, while striding forward with a rifle strapped to her back.

"Then mine is going right beside her," Perri replied softly as she held up a photograph to the wall. She had always been drawn to the sculpture depicting a slender young woman in a stovepipe bonnet that cut off most of her vision. The woman held a baby at her hip while taking the rifle from her husband, who lay dying at her feet.

Looking at the photographs instilled a feeling of heart and courage. "We'll make the wall of the Pioneer Women our own now." She paused for a moment to take a deep breath and to contain the tears. "And by this time tomorrow, Matt Ransom will know he's going to be a father," Perri vowed, daring to look to the future.

"Get in," he said.

Lida Kell scrambled awkwardly onto the passenger seat of the pickup, her usual glamorous self a soggy mess. "Thanks, Matt," she said breathlessly. "That was a scary one. I'm pretty sure it's just the battery, but the hail cracked my windshield. I'm grateful to you for stopping."

The brutal hailstorm had forced images of Cadie once more onto his shoulders. Matt had felt the need to get out and drive once the hail had quit. Just as he had had to stop and offer assistance when he'd found her. A woman alone in a storm would always tear at him. *Even if it is Lida Kell,* he thought, as he grimly resumed the drive to his own residence on the Ransom place.

Lida chattered nonstop about some property out by Spirit Lake. She had met a buyer out there, if he'd caught that part correctly. Anyway, he had come upon her car practically in the ditch. *The wrong place at the wrong time,* he mused.

Matt now thoroughly regretted that he had gone out to the lake to think. He should have stayed home. But something was not quite right with Perri, and it was gnawing at him.

Of course, a large part of it was that they hadn't had sex since their wedding night. It was obviously the lack of sex after such a night that was getting to him. After all, he didn't have any emotions, any finer feelings left in him. It certainly couldn't be love for Perri; just a potent blend of lust and business.

The storm-whipped water had been a sight. It had helped him immensely to witness the turmoil. The lake had looked the way he was feeling about the situation with his wife. It wasn't serious, of course. It was just that Matt hadn't touched her in too long.

Here, he had gone out of his way for a whole month to be considerate and polite, and Perri still hadn't come around. And now the local spider woman was going to destroy his reflective mood. He smiled briefly at Lida to convince her he was listening.

Matt had noted long ago that Lida Kell was not an intelligent woman. She was however, bulldog tenacious. She had, at one time on her journey through life, come upon that famous quote about persistence paying and had taken it to heart. She had figured correctly that her looks, coupled with a will of iron, were her strongest approach.

Now at the ripe old age of twenty-eight, she seemed to care about proving she could be something other that an intricately designed, prettily polished toy. And she was just stupid enough and brazen enough to be very dangerous.

She'd gotten her real estate agent's license shortly after her divorce. Matt shuddered at the thought. Lida seemed hell-bent to establish herself as a player responsible for turning Spirit Valley into even more of a bedroom community, further leeching vitality from the town. She probably already had planned which power suit she was going to wear to the closing if Gannie's land got turned over to the developers. The woman tended to keep her eye on the essentials.

If Matt couldn't stop her, he imagined she'd see to it that the condo's parking lot and dumpsite spilled over into his pasture. She had not been best pleased when he had declined her generous, sexual offer after Cadie's death. Matt had politely explained that he didn't mess with married women. Especially not women married to men he had known since kindergarten.

Even if he hadn't been dead set against it, it brought thoughts of his grandfather and the old scandal too much to mind. He had tactfully refrained from telling Lida it was also because she made him feel even more dead inside than he already did.

He now made an effort to tune the woman in, as he realized she was chattering on about Gannie's project. And about Perri. Matt was struck once again by the way she giggled. She sounded almost exactly like his late wife. He took a deep breath, convinced this short but wearying drive from the lake was carrying him closer to sainthood.

I don't suppose I could just shoot her, he thought ruefully. "Come on in, Lida," Matt said, pulling up by his front porch, "and dry off. When the storm quits, we'll see about your car."

Five

"I guess you missed the hail. At least you'd better tell me you missed it," Matt said evenly as he met Perri on his front porch. "It was heavy. I'd like to think you wouldn't try to drive through something like that."

As she smiled and came forward to kiss him, Matt realized how much her pulling away had left him needing to see her here. To witness Perri willingly striding toward him on Ransom land. Her ability to retreat from him, to regain her distance, had left him feeling rather desperate. He braced himself and tried not to think of how desperate he was to get through the next five minutes.

"I hope I'm not intruding," she said as she shivered in the chilly wind. "The weather was so weird, I kept driving in from Oklahoma City just to see what it would do. Mom sends her best, by the way. Anyway, when I got past Gledhill, I thought I'd stop by for a minute." Perri halted abruptly. She was babbling. "I did miss the hail, Matt," she added, smiling up at him. "But it's been so long since I've driven through a bright, sunny rainstorm, I just had to be out in it. I'd forgotten how pretty it could be.

"Look," she continued, running her hand up to the collar of his shirt, "I don't want to impose on your work. I just thought if you would like to invite your father over for dinner—"

Perri's voice tapered off as she heard Lida Kell struggle with a fit of the giggles through the open front door. Her gaze moved beyond Matt for a more thorough inspection. Perri's mouth twitched once before she set her features into neutral. "Hello, Lida," she said politely.

Something in her tone, coupled with the knowing look in those pretty eyes, had his head whipping around. Matt's features sharpened. He watched helplessly as Lida slowly made it to the screen door, clearly naked except for one of his shirts.

"Oops," Lida said with a smirk and another giggle, as Matt's grip on his wife tightened.

Fury pounded through him for an instant before it was replaced by patient weariness. "Your timing is perfect," he sighed, returning his gaze to Perri. "If you'll bring her out to the lake when she's decent, by the time you get there, I should have her battery recharged. Don't say it," Matt ordered, squeezing her, as Perri bit back a retort about Lida ever being "decent" and "recharging batteries."

"And watch her while she dresses, will you? Check her purse, if you can," he murmured, kissing her cheek. "Now don't start!" he ordered when he felt her begin to break up.

"Please don't make me watch her dress," Perri begged as she battled for composure. "Anything but that!"

"She's asked too many questions about the project," Matt whispered. "I don't want to find a disk missing on that survey work we just had done, okay?" He patted Perri's bottom before heading for his pickup. "Oh, and darlin'," he added casually as he rounded the cab. "Toss that shirt she's wearing in the trash for me, will you?"

It doesn't matter, she told herself. *All that matters is the baby and the land.* Perri emphasized each thought with the slam of a pot or pan. She paused from stirring the chili con queso, made from scratch, and turned to take the chili cheese ball out of the fridge.

Obviously she hadn't been thinking to make them both. But, hey, she hadn't killed Lida Kell either. Matt would just have to live on cheese for one night. She was in such a mood.

What she had really not been in the mood for, of course, was the sight of Lida's fabulously tanned, silky smooth body in one of Matt's shirts. And now, she was really in no mood to discuss impending parenthood with the father-to-be.

"It doesn't matter what he wants or what he thinks, or how he feels about it," she said out loud to the lonely kitchen. She slammed the chili cheese ball onto a platter. "It can't matter. All that matters is the baby."

Pouring the con queso into an electric fondue pot, Perri practically threw the ancient pan into the sink. "I *want* it to matter," she declared through tensely gritted teeth. "I want it to matter to him. I want it to matter that *I'm* his wife. That I'm the one having his child.

"Don't you dare make it easy, Perri Ransom," she lectured herself. "You made it easy on Leila. That's half of what's got you steamed now, isn't it? Too much the lady, the good daughter, to fight that witch full out. Well, now you've got something worth fighting for. You've got a marriage," she scolded herself, "such as it is, and a baby coming."

Crossing to turn the steaks in their marinade, she absently checked the temperature gauge outside the kitchen window. It really had dropped twenty-five degrees in two hours. *Welcome to Tornado Alley,* she reflected. That's when she saw him. Perri had to remind herself to breathe.

Matt took a good, wary look at his wife before centering his attention upon the lethal-looking red football on the kitchen counter. "What is that thing?" he inquired, fascinated in spite of himself.

"A chili cheese ball," Perri enunciated as she practically threw a bag of tortilla chips at him.

"Oh good Lord."

"So don't eat it," she replied curtly. "Instead, perhaps you could tell me if Lida was a strategy to get me off the dime. Because it more or less worked."

"Lida was dressed when she excused herself to use the facilities and I headed out onto the porch to greet you, Perri," he replied. The truth was he wouldn't touch Lida Kell with a pitchfork. "And besides, you didn't seem too upset," Matt pointed out as he grabbed a bowl and opened the chips.

"As I recall, you were close to laughing the whole time I worked on her battery." He couldn't help but smile. "I must say, hon," he added, "I admired the way you managed to annoy her while remaining so very ladylike about it. That was quite a sight."

"And you were expecting what, Matt?" she demanded. "A catfight at the OK Corral? Please. You would never shame me that way. Nor would you willingly bring someone like that onto your own place."

"Thank you," he said, his attention focused solely on Perri. In the stillness she created he studied her, savoring a sense of relief. She understood about Lida. And that was the only thing that mattered.

Suddenly he knew. He just knew, with absolute certainty why she had been hanging onto herself so hard. Matt's nostrils flared like a stallion's as his body went on the alert. He could almost scent the truth. "You're pregnant, aren't you, Perri?" he asked quietly, mirroring her repose.

"Yes, Matt, I am," she said, head high, eyes meeting his.

He moved with deceptive speed. But even when he had her pinned to the door of the fridge, Perri never broke his gaze or registered any alarm. She silently gave in to his greater strength, absorbing it. Matt palmed her chin, pressing the back of her head into the shiny surface of the door. He saw Perri witness his momentary flash of triumph before he quickly damped it down.

In the stillness, the truth in her was palpable. Matt didn't want to injure that. He would have to be very careful with her and with his own rage, he reasoned. He held his emotions and body in check like a bronc ready to burst from the chute. "Why haven't you told me?" His tone was low and savage.

Matt watched as puzzlement drifted through the emerald shards in Perri's eyes, just before she lost all patience with him.

"Oh, for heaven's sake, Matt, you can count! How long do you think I've even suspected I should buy a home test? 'Why haven't you told me?''' she mimicked. "What do you think I was doing on your doorstep this afternoon? What else would be important enough for me to interrupt your work?" she demanded.

She looked right at him and barreled on. "Would you have preferred I brought the matter up in front of Lida?" she demanded, her hands moving to his biceps. "Should I have waited until after I had her stuffed back into that ridiculous suit? Or would you have been overjoyed if I'd gone ahead and given you the news when she was standing just about naked at your front door? Are you questioning my—"

"Okay!" Matt slapped both palms against the door on either side of her head. He caged her, breathing hard. "When do you see the doctor?" he demanded.

"In two days," she stated flatly.

"You're going tomorrow," he volleyed back.

"I'm going in two days," she repeated, getting more annoyed. "By then my medical records should be here. It can wait two days to confirm the home test, Matt."

Matt stared deeply into her eyes. The woman didn't seem to have enough sense to be afraid of him. "You are taking perfect care of this baby, understand?" It was an intimidation.

"Well of course I am," she said in exasperation. "Matt, it will be fine. Women have been having babies for some time now."

"And women have been having miscarriages. Just as women have been having abortions," he answered, grabbing her shoulders. "And you're not having one this time. Do you hear me? *This* time you are having my baby." He couldn't help but shake her, just once to make his point. "Don't even think about taking that road again, Perri."

"What are you talking about?" she demanded, suddenly suspicious. She grabbed onto his shirt. It was clear now that more was driving him than she had realized or anticipated.

"I'm not talking. I'm telling you. You aren't having an abortion this time," he stated in cold, clipped tones. "You're having my baby. Don't even think about an alternative."

"Of course I'm not having an abortion. I would never have an abortion, Matt," her voice filled with hurt and bewilderment. "You ought to know that. It's taken me this long to get married and pregnant. You needn't act as if you have to demand that I go through with this pregnancy. I'm having this baby, with or without you. Matt!" she yelped as this time his fingers dug into her jaw.

Her response was shaking him. Matt could almost feel the floor turn to dust under his feet. The foundation on which he had built the last twelve years was finally called into question. "Perri, so help me. Don't lie to me! Not now," he ordered, his tone murderous. "I know you aborted my baby after you settled in Raleigh—"

"What are you talking about?" She slapped his hands away as her fury took hold. "I would never abort a baby."

"I know how young you were and I can understand—"

"There's nothing for you to understand except that that is a lie!" she shouted. "You always took care of protection, Matt. You were very careful with me. Don't you remember?" The truth in her words seemed to finally reach this stranger who still had her pinned. "Where did you get this ridiculous notion that I was ever pregnant at seventeen?"

Her query froze him into an animal-like stillness. That she would get so exasperated led him to think. "My mother," he answered hoarsely. *His mother.* He had never examined the source.

Perri froze, as Matt's statement clicked into place. "Of course," she whispered as the realization hit home. It took her a moment to continue. She looked him right in the eye and willed the truth into her voice. "It never happened, Matt," she declared solemnly. "I swear it."

And he believed her. "You're telling me you didn't abort our child twelve years ago?" he asked carefully, his voice dried out by shock. He couldn't wrap his mind around what would haunt him more: If the woman caged in his arms was lying to him or telling him the truth. Either way, there was no turning back now.

"I wasn't pregnant twelve years ago," she stated simply, fighting through her sorrow. "I've never been pregnant in my life."

The truth was too close to the surface for him not to see it. Matt released Perri and pushed off the refrigerator door. He had to get away from her, and from Gledhill, before his rage tore apart what was left between them.

But first, he took the time to really look at her in the stillness. Then he grimly turned and headed for his pickup.

Matt was pulling out before she could bring herself to breathe. Perri remained still and absorbed the soft, reassuring hum of the refrigerator against her back. It felt almost human. Certainly more human than the savage eyes that had pinned her to its door.

Where could he go, he wondered. *Where?* For once in his life, Matt stopped at every stop sign and stoplight on his way through Spirit Valley. Each stop was punctuated with the same question: *Where* could he go? Where could he take the tempest within him to play it out with the least destruction?

He was driving through the entrance to the cemetery and parking in front of a gray marble bench, before he knew what hit him. Matt figured it probably said something important that he found himself drawn to Gannie's grave instead of one of his blood kin. But he just wasn't the type of man to dwell upon whatever the significance might be.

He bent down by the curb to uproot some weeds that the mower had missed. Matt reluctantly lifted his eyes for a moment and sighed before focusing back on the curb. Today was not the first time that the view from the center of the cemetery had left him feeling choked and suffocated.

This part of Oklahoma was so flat. Usually the flatness caused a mirage, fooling the observer into thinking everything was a great distance away. But for the moment in the crisp, chilly air the town, the grain elevator and the Interstate all seemed to rise up and shadow the graves. The spirits of Spirit Valley seemed to call out: "This, then, is the result of your toil."

Cold summer wind marked this day as out of the ordinary.

Normally, it was hot enough to scald the brain. *San Francisco weather,* he thought idly just before the truth hit him. He stood up abruptly and faced the newly laid stone. "You knew!" he whispered to Gannie's grave. "You knew she was never pregnant."

And so should have you, Matt, came the thought in answer to his discovery. Well. He hunkered back down to the curb, stunned. Anyone passing would have witnessed one of the Ransoms pulling weeds by Gannie's grave and thought nothing of it. Other than to admire the industry. The man whose strong hands tidied up the curb did not resemble someone reviewing the consequences of never having sought out the truth for himself.

After a time, Matt got back in his pickup and started for home. He knew the truth now and it made him sick. It was going to be all but impossible to offer up amends for something that had hurt them both to the bone. But he owed Perri that much, at least, for his behavior. Behavior based on the lies of the past.

What other lies had his mother told him? he wondered. He would have to find out what other hurts he needed to mend. It was a painful task, but anything less wouldn't do.

Matt's vehicle thundered over the railroad tracks, its driver unaware that for the first time he had thought of Gledhill as "home." When he arrived, Perri was gone.

For once, there was no evening wind. The chill and the silence made it feel like a different world. Perri opened the back door to the porch and froze. She hadn't seen him through the windows. Matt sat in the gathering darkness with his feet propped on the rim of the hot tub and a bottle on the floor next to his chair.

"Where have you been?" he inquired softly.

"The same place you've been," she countered. "Out."

He turned to look at her. Suddenly, she recalled a photo she'd seen in a New York paper. It was the cheekbones that had drawn her eye to the man's face in the first place. With hawklike nose and brows, coupled with a quality of utter stillness, the young father in the photograph had reminded her of Matt.

The picture had been taken during the aftermath of a sniper's random violence. A man had been photographed sitting in a police car, having received the news that his wife and two little girls were dead from sniper fire.

He wasn't crying or grieving publicly in any way. Instead, it was as if his grief had frozen; as if the imploded emotion had shattered some internal structure. All that seemed to hold him upright was the block of ice that had formed where his feelings had once resided. Feelings now buried too deep to surface.

She had seen the front-page photo at a newsstand on her way to the subway. It had mentally propelled her back home in an instant. *Matt*, she had thought, standing in front of the subway kiosk as the morning straphangers had swirled around her in the real world. He looked so much like that photo now.

Perri watched him pull in the reins on his sorrow and decide to focus on what would matter.

"We need to talk," he announced as he lifted the bottle.

"Okay," she said, all business. "I'll begin. Let me ask the obvious, Matt. Do you have any proof that I had an abortion?" she inquired solemnly. "And please explain this to me—How would Leila know that I was pregnant?"

The words formed reluctantly. "She said you called her from Raleigh and asked her to pay for an abortion of my baby," he answered.

"And you believed her? Of course. What am I saying?" she muttered bitterly. "But why? Why would I call that woman for anything? You, of all people, knew I had money of my own."

She observed Matt suddenly remember. The only fights they'd ever had, had been over Perri's insisting she could work instead of going on to college.

"Remember, Matt? My dowry?" she smiled sadly as she thought back to another time. "I actually thought of the money I had saved as my dowry. I thought it was so romantic. How could I ever have been that young?" she asked, bewildered. "Lord, I was so proud. Having my own money made me feel so very grown-up, so in command of my future. After all, I knew how to make a living."

She looked at him for a long moment as the tears formed.

"And that pride surely did precede my fall," she said softly. "It meant so much to me that I had earned that money." Perri's sorrowful chuckle hung between them. "It meant so much to me that I had something solid to bring to our marriage, in case your parents cut you off. Something to help us get started.

"I had more than enough money to pay for my own abortion," she continued briskly, "if I were someone who would have considered such an alternative. *If* I had been pregnant.

"And the Matt I loved then knew me well enough to know I would never have taken that road," she said with conviction. She moved to lean against the hot tub. "If you want to take it further, why would I go to Leila?" she asked. "I could have asked you, or just shown up pregnant at your wedding."

Perri turned to face him. "Do you really think that the one person on earth I would have asked would have been your mother? Especially after she blackmailed me out of town?"

"After she *what?*" he demanded, pushing out of the chair. "What else do I need to know? Say it." Matt stood his ground and waited to hear the worst.

"Leila threatened to start a rumor to ruin my mother's business," Perri said as she turned in the darkness toward the west. There, threads of pink and coral still glowed on the darkening horizon. "She threatened to spread it around that Sam was having an affair with my mom if I didn't leave for Raleigh right away. If I didn't stay away from you." Perri sighed. "Leila declaring publicly that Mom was Sam's mistress was too awful for me to contemplate. When Mom moved to Oklahoma City, she did it because she wanted to expand her business, not because your mother ran her out of town. Leila made it clear to me she would have enjoyed ruining my mother's reputation. I couldn't let that happen, Matt," Perri added.

"But he *was* having an affair with Janie," Matt responded.

"No, he wasn't, Matt," Perri declared forcefully.

He didn't need light. He could feel her gaze pin him in the dark.

"And how do you know that, anyway? Is that what your father said?" Perri paused long enough to give him an opportunity to speak. He didn't. "You never asked Sam, did you? Have you ever asked him anything? Have you ever questioned any of it?'' she demanded, her voice rising. ''The truth has been right in your own home all the time, and you never asked your father to confirm or deny it, did you?''

''Mom begged me not to ask him, not to hurt her pride,'' Matt said, his heart sickening as he realized he had cut his father out of his life without ever giving the man a chance.

''Well, of course she did,'' Perri replied in weary exasperation. ''Not that it's any of my business, but why don't you ask your father now, Matt?'' she challenged. ''Ask him if there's any truth to the ugly, damaging rumor that my mother was his mistress. While you're at it, ask Sam if he has any ideas as to how Leila could possibly have found out I was pregnant.

''Your mother was here to see me at Gledhill that night, just before you came by to break my heart.'' Matt flinched at her words, but said nothing. ''Her threats to harm my mother's reputation are what successfully ran a seventeen-year-old girl out of town. The choice came down to you or my mother.''

Perri stopped. She was suddenly struck by the knowledge that the choice had been the same for both of them. They had both chosen in favor of family. ''At this moment,'' she said, ''more than ever, I know I made the correct decision. Did you ever question your mother, Matt?''

Her inquiry was answered by a long, painful silence. ''Well,'' Perri sighed, ''perhaps we can put this situation into the proper perspective. If I can tough it out under the same roof with you, if I'm determined to keep this small corner of our mutual heritage intact, then surely you can make a similar effort. You're going to be a father, Matt,'' she added, ''or at least you have fathered a baby.''

''I was rough on you that night,'' Matt stated simply. ''Words are not enough. But I am sorry. I'm terribly sorry.''

No, words were not enough. He didn't love her, and she was having his child. Perri relived the triumph she'd seen in his eyes when he'd realized she was pregnant. ''It's always going to be there between us, isn't it, Matt? Well, just think of me as a broodmare of dubious bloodlines,'' she said sadly.

''Perri,'' Matt began, ''there's something *you* need to know.

The only reason I asked Cadie to marry me, and went through with it so fast, is because I believed Leila.''

Perri turned from him and headed into the kitchen without another word. There was nothing more to be said.

"You hurt her and I'll make you pay for it, Ransom," Perri's father had warned over the phone, shortly before the wedding.

"Understood, sir," Matt had replied respectfully. It was best not to mess with Mike Stone. "Fair enough. As to that," he'd continued, "I have a feeling my own father would probably beat you to it."

"Oh, no," Mike had stated with quick conviction. "Tell Sam if anything happens to Perri, you're mine."

Matt knew Mike would give him no second chance. He now knew he wouldn't deserve it.

He probably shouldn't inflict himself on the three people now gathered in his father's house. But welcome or merely tolerated, he wouldn't let Perri face Sam and Janie without him. Matt pulled the car into the driveway next to Janie's and got out. For a moment he paused to review the events of the morning. Events that had led Janie Stone's car to now occupy Sam Ransom's driveway.

Matt had accompanied Perri to her doctor's appointment, where Dr. Berkka had confirmed her pregnancy. He had made it through the consultation solely on stoic resolve. No one would have known that Matt Ransom had anything more on his mind than adjusting to the fact that he was soon to be a daddy.

But Janie had met them at the doctor's office and Perri had driven off with her mother. He had come home alone. And the silence of Gledhill had mocked him. Matt had had one task to complete before heading out to track them down. He'd known instinctively where to look. Matt had figured from her mood that his wife just might have some questions of her own about the past. It was easy to reason out where she might go for some answers. He headed for the front door.

Well, let's get it done, he thought grimly, entering the old Ransom place. He could only hope he would be welcome.

Perri turned her head and regarded him as he appeared in the doorway of Sam's office. "I didn't say anything you don't already know," she declared. "Sam has kindly agreed to help clear the air."

The emerald silk suited her, Matt noticed. The simple style of the campshirt and matching pants looked easy, elegant and very right on her willowy frame. It certainly brought out the green in those oddly colored eyes.

She'd done something different to her hair and to her face. Matt had never seen her look like this. It was certainly a more sophisticated, more formal Perri and it hadn't even registered on him earlier in the day.

Mine. The random, unwanted thought gave him pause. His gut tightened in a possessive moment. Perri looked like a woman who was prepared to assert herself if necessary. Prepared to take a stand. And then he caught the look on his father's face.

Sam Ransom had always appreciated a good-looking woman with long legs and a fluid, easy walk. Perri seemed as yet unaware that somewhere between the wedding and today, she had made a conquest.

A look arced from father to son. Matt grinned at his dad.

No comment passed between them, but Sam slowly smiled back. Something had been mended; they both felt it.

Matt nodded to his father in silent and grateful understanding.

Sam nodded in return from behind his desk as his oldest son entered. "Take a seat, since you're here. I was just explaining to Perri that I used to worry so much about my mother trying to hurt Janie, I barely paid attention to the damage my wife could cause," Sam said. He settled in to explain some things to Janie's girl.

"My mother was one hell of an adversary, Perri," he said, "especially when she thought my father was unfaithful to her." Sam stopped and smiled at Janie when she couldn't hold back a sigh. "Mama didn't have it in her to be forgiving. It's something to have to live with, when your mother takes a shot at your father."

"Luckily for Dad, he moved as she aimed," Sam chuckled ruefully, "because my mother's intention was to shatter his kneecap. He was only creased, but Dad got the point. He figured the scandal would be worse if he stayed."

"Can you explain something, Sam?" Perri asked. "He—Grandpa Larry—never pressed charges did he?"

"Against his wife?" Sam asked. "Of course not!"

The look on her face made it clear that further explanation was in order.

"It was only a crease. And besides, your great-uncle Marlowe was the law, and old Doc Berkka was the doctor. Everybody agreed it was just a hunting accident," he said calmly.

Perri stared at him and huffed out a disgusted breath.

"Well, it was a hunting accident," Matt added patiently. "The accident was, that she only creased him. She had planned to do a lot more damage than that. Grandma was aiming to shatter his kneecap when he moved out of her line of fire." And by his lights, that was that.

"Now, Dad swore that he and your grandmother had never acted upon their mutual attraction," Sam went on, "but still it hurt my mother's pride. Her own actions drove Dad to protect and defend your grandmother."

This was the part that was so difficult to admit. "He took your grandmother away from here because he was afraid my mother might kill her. And," Sam couldn't keep the yearning out of his voice, "he took Anne away from Spirit because he loved her. Still does, I understand."

"Why wasn't I told before now that Mrs. Ransom shot him, Mom?" Perri inquired in a tight little voice.

Janie grimaced. "That was just bad timing, Perri. We didn't know quite how to go about it. You were finally getting old enough to ask for the details when you fell in love with Matt," she explained. "I got it into my head that Larry should be the one to tell you, but he was reluctant. He thought you were still too young. I thought he was wrong," Janie added, "but I was dealing with other problems. It was so soon after my divorce.

"I believe Larry was afraid you'd think less of him, or of your grandmother, and that he'd lose you," she reflected. "Just as he'd lost Sam."

Perri looked owlishly at her mother. "Well, it was a little awkward," Janie said defensively. "We sort of figured one day you'd ask Grandpa how he hurt his leg and we'd take it from there."

Matt was staring at Janie, finally looking beneath the surface of his own suppositions. "Grandma would have destroyed Anne Marlowe if given half a chance," he said slowly as the realization took hold. It didn't need saying what she would have done if Sam had married Janie, as intended at the time.

Sam nodded in quick agreement and continued. "So, out of loyalty to my mother, I married Leila. And that was another set of worries. Mama never let Leila forget about Janie and me," he said. "She saw to it that the wound never healed for either of us. Me, it just made my sense of duty to my family that much stronger. What else was there to do? This Ransom wasn't going to get a divorce. But just as my own mother was one hell of an adversary," he added, "so was Leila."

No one in the room argued the point.

"I should have known when Leila started crying so hysterically that night, that she was planning to work Matt over," Sam went on. "My wife so seldom cried. It was a terrifying sight whenever she did."

"I walked out on Matt," Sam admitted, "when his mother started in on him. Even though I felt I should have advised him to end your relationship, Perri, I just couldn't do it. I'm sorry, Perri, Janie," Sam said gazing at each of them in turn. "I wasn't there for him when he needed me. I know now I should never have left it up to his mother."

Sam paused, taking a close and careful reading of whether or not now was the right time. "Now I hope y'all will stay for lunch," he added graciously.

The amused, knowing look in those black eyes made Perri smile at the polite offer. *No wonder my mom was a goner over this one*, she thought dryly. Perri realized she had fallen in love with Sam Ransom. "Thank you, Sam," she said, meaning it.

"It's time we made things easy, honey," Sam replied.

It was Janie's turn. "Thank you, Sam, that's kind of you," she said as she rose from the chair. "But I seem to have no appetite. I think I'll just go on," Janie added as she headed for the door.

She paused when she reached her son-in-law and watched while he rose respectfully to his feet. "Matt, for the record—I've never been your father's mistress, nor has he ever asked me to consider such a thing.

"Now," she continued firmly. "You and I have to see each other, at least occasionally, because of Perri. You are, after all, the father of my grandbaby. I hope this matter is finally cleared up for you," she declared. "I don't want to have to deal with this sort of misunderstanding after today."

Misunderstanding, Matt thought. The woman had a way with understatements. "I'd like to take this opportunity to apologize to you and to Perri," he said formally. "Janie, it's clear to me I acted on incorrect information and behaved badly. I'm heartily sorry for the damage I've done."

Janie nodded her assent. It was a start and enough for now. The women departed, leaving the Ransom house missing something important. Something Matt had never before noticed it lacked.

The men listened to the car pulling out of the drive. "Why didn't you ask me, Matt? I would have told you the truth," Sam said wearily. "I guess I'm grateful to now at least understand why you shut me out after that night."

"I couldn't ask you for the truth, not at the time. Now I have amends to make," Matt sighed, "I don't deny it."

"Son," Sam began, "last time I stayed out of it to my ever-lasting regret. But Perri doesn't have a father here to speak to you. So I'm giving you warning that I'm taking on the job," Sam declared. "If you are careless with her, if you hurt her, so help me I will hold you down myself until Mike Stone can get here from Raleigh and take his best shot." Sam paused to let the words sink in. "Now go do right by your wife."

"We need to mend fences, Dad," Matt answered. "But you're right. I have to see to Perri first. She's what's most important now," he added softly.

Sam started out the door, leaving Matt to ponder how it must have been for him to witness his woman marry another man. "I'm so sorry," Matt whispered, staring after his father.

Six

Could they become a family? Could it be done through sheer force of will? Matt pondered such questions as he watched his mother-in-law go about Gledhill's miniature graveyard without so much as a glance in his direction. After placing a Sonia rose on the marker inscribed *Stone Baby 1889*, Janie Stone dusted off her hands and moved back to her car. Matt stood on the front porch and watched her departure, contemplating exactly what he was going to do about the newest abyss between himself and his wife.

So. What does this baby mean to a six-month marriage? he wondered as he journeyed up the stairs. Turning toward the bedroom, Matt realized he knew the answer to at least one of the questions drifting around in his mind. He didn't want his marriage to end in six months. He wanted them to continue on as a family.

Being Matt Ransom, he didn't pause to reflect on why he might want to keep Perri as his wife. Instead, his finely tuned skills at strategy quickly worked out how best to present this change of heart and get her to agree.

What kind of a husband can I be to her? Matt wondered as he entered the master bedroom. He paused as his gaze fell upon her. She didn't look particularly delighted to see him.

Turning to search his face for answers of her own, Perri said nothing. She grimly stood by the brass bed and watched him remove the sportcoat he had worn for their appointment with the doctor. His dress shirt had made its way to the doorknob of the closet before she finally found her voice. "I am not thrilled about this," she stated, gesturing around the room.

The man had already given her such a headache, just looking at him hurt. Perri gingerly lifted the back of her neck. If she could just get the pain at the back of her head to let up, maybe the pounding in her temples would lessen as well.

Perri scolded herself into not throwing something at him. Matt had been careful, even methodical, she noted as she looked around. He hadn't just dumped her stuff in his room. He had paid attention to what he was doing with her property when he'd moved her things out of the little bedroom facing the backyard.

He had certainly been busy in the interval between the doctor's and Sam's. Even the humidor for his occasional cigars had thoughtfully disappeared. Matt had truly made an effort to subdue his own presence upon the space.

Some thought had gone into the way he had hung her clothes in his closet, and how he'd carefully placed her clock and journal on top of the nightstand. It looked as if a swift but determined effort had been made to create a shared bedroom.

"Perhaps you'd be kind enough to explain why my things have been moved in here," she stated waspishly. "Is this your subtle way of telling me that we're going to be sleeping together?" Now her shoulders were beginning to throb. Her eyes definitely felt smaller and filled with grit. Perri hugged herself and started for the door. Matt immediately blocked her.

"Please put everything—"

"You have a headache, don't you?" he asked softly. "You need an ice pack. I'll get it," he said, gently leading her to that enormous brass bed. "Let me," he urged, quiet but determined.

Perri lay on the bed and watched him solemnly remove her shoes. Matt rubbed her arms and hands. She batted fretfully at him when he began to unbutton her blouse. "I'm just going to massage your neck and shoulders," he said, ignoring her efforts. "Come on, honey, on your stomach."

Feeling slightly foolish, Perri sighed dramatically, removed her blouse and turned to grip the ornate brass bars in stoic obedience. Matt chuckled as he gently caressed where neck and skull joined. The way he proceeded to slowly stroke the column of her neck didn't really qualify as massage, but she didn't mention it. His hand was so warm, so familiar. His strength so real. Her breathing was beginning to shorten, and her fingers curled more tightly around the brass.

Perri bit back a moan as he slowly began to work on her shoulders. A tiny spark of heat flickered low in her belly, growing steadily. She sighed, remembering. He had always had such great hands. And even though he used them now only to soothe, she knew he could feel her bones begin to melt. She fought the impulse to curve into his touch.

"That's right, hon. That's good." He patted her bottom easily. "I'll be right back," he said, pulling on a dark green T-shirt. He found an afghan to cover her against the air conditioner's chill before heading toward the hall.

Matt and a baby. The look of triumph he had quickly damped down when he had pinned her to the fridge the other day had confirmed something she'd known intuitively. Matt wanted this baby. And he needed a caretaker for that child. So, for the present at least, he considered her essential. Her husband might not love her, but he knew he needed her. She realized she hadn't let go of the bars.

As it welled up within her, the overwhelming desire she felt to have Matt's baby brought tears to her eyes. She had always slammed down on, danced away from such need before. The need for this, this child. Wanting Matt's baby had been the source of her continuing to run. She could see that now. The combination of unacknowledged longing and actively moving on had kept the past preserved. *No wonder I never married.* The thought came uninvited.

A new generation. A Stone-Ransom baby. The thought of it caused her throat to close. The child would have to be told how it all came about. *A child of love,* she thought fiercely, knowing she would always make that clear. What she and Matt were doing to preserve Gledhill gave this baby a special heritage. It made them a part of the claim upon this land.

Well, they were going to have to talk about what would happen when the six months were up. They would have to think of the baby. Perri had never felt a greater need for Gannie's strength and wisdom than she did at the moment. She could hear Matt ascending the stairs.

He came in with an ice pack and a damp towel. She rolled over onto her back and studied him a little warily as he tended to her needs. "How did you know?" she inquired softly. "How did you know so suddenly that I was pregnant?"

"I've known you a long time, hon," he remarked as he gently settled the back of her head against the ice pack. "All I really had to do was to see what was in front of my eyes. That's all." He paused briefly as he realized how inapt that remark sounded, in light of what he had learned about his mother.

"And the food projects," he added as an afterthought. She looked puzzled. "Per, you made chili con queso and that cheese football-thing at the same time." He breathed an exaggerated sigh in response to her look. "Am I the only one here who knows anything about being pregnant?" Matt asked. He chuckled as she glared at him. "Figures."

Matt reached into the drawer of the nightstand and pulled out a little velvet box. "I want you to have this, hon," he said softly. "It belongs to you. I've kept it for you a long time."

Perri had to swallow hard as she silently took the box from him. Opening it, she carefully removed the familiar locket. It weighed with the years between them as it rested in her hand. She could barely look at it; it meant too much. "Thank you, Matt. That was thoughtful of you," she said formally. Somehow, even though the air-conditioning cooled the room, the necklace burned her with remorse.

Perri gripped the locket tightly, as if she could physically grasp hold of a second chance. Was there a way, ever, to bring love back to what it had been? Especially when it was clearly being forced into existence through duty?

"Last time you wore it, it meant we were engaged," he said as her eyes got even bigger. The green glints did not contain their usual clarity.

Twelve years lost, he thought sadly. Matt had wondered how to go about giving back the antique locket. It signified so much hope and despair. He watched as unwittingly Perri touched her throat.

The fragile, involuntary movement went through him like a knife. When he had stormed into Gledhill and broken up with her that dreadful night, he had grabbed the chain as if to rip it off. The only thing that had kept it from breaking had been the fact that it was so heavy. The gold necklace was plain enough not to attract much notice. But inside, the locket sheltered a small diamond. Her hand moved with regret from her throat as he carefully pressed the damp towel to her forehead.

"Perri." Nerves had him clearing his throat. He couldn't do anything about the awkwardness. "I would like to see a future that means more than horses and hard work," Matt said quietly. "Whenever I've thought of you, secretly dreamed of you, you've always symbolized family and home to me. And I want that. I want this marriage to continue past the six-month arrangement."

The very air seemed to still at his words. Matt could see he had her full attention, even through the pain of her headache. She froze, staring hard into his eyes. "I want that very much," he said. "I don't think I have much to give you. But I want a chance for something that doesn't feel like it's covered in dust." It took him some time to continue. "Can we make it work?" he asked softly. "Can you forgive me?"

"I can forgive you," Perri said simply and without hesitation.

Matt stroked her hair as he searched her eyes. "How can you forgive so easily, Perri?" he asked.

"You're the father of my child, Matt," she replied. "And I love you. And most importantly, I want it done. I want it behind us so I don't have to be pregnant with the past over me and my baby."

Matt desperately wished he could tell her that he loved her. But it hurt even to try. The anguish that accompanied each attempt to express love just about ripped him apart.

So far, each attempt had been brought to a halt by the sickening realization that there was nothing down inside where heart, soul and loving feelings were said to reside. The insight brought a tight, sad feeling to his chest and throat. A feral wariness came over him as he searched inside himself once again for some feelings of love.

There had to be some love in him, didn't there? It couldn't all have been reduced to duty and sexual desire. If that proved to be the truth, then his mother had won. And by damn, he didn't want that to happen. He reached for Perri. He had to hold her.

Cradling her in his arms, Matt buried his face at her throat. "Then we'll call it done," he said finally, moved by the ease with which she had declared her love. "And as I told you back then, to me the old scandal over our grandparents was just that. Old news. When I asked you to marry me, I didn't really understand how serious it was to Mom. Not that I gave a damn," he added more calmly.

He stroked her hair and allowed the familiar scent of her skin to soothe his heart. "I loved you too much to care. I'm sorry, Perri. I really believed everything she told me that night," he vowed. "I swear it.

"I cut myself off from my father the same night I cut you loose. And I never told him what was wrong," he added, sorrow in every word. "He was so bewildered with me. I hurt my father. And I hurt you." Perri felt the muscles in his arms bunch, as, on an involuntary movement he gathered her even more tightly to him. In that moment her heart broke for him.

"When I think of how it must have felt, listening to my accusations. Well, I'm just grateful you can forgive me." Matt's eyes, for once, seemed almost black enough to give off light rather than to absorb it.

"Matt," she began, "why did you move my things in here?" She could feel his body tense.

"Because you're the mother of my child. And because." It cost him to continue. "I'd like to explain further," he said, "but I'm just no good at this."

"You used to be," she replied simply, without any intensity

to the words. Only the force with which she still clutched the locket betrayed any emotion.

"Well, I'm not," he answered. "I don't know how anymore. Maybe with you, I could learn." Matt paused to study her closely, checking to make sure she was all right. "I'll let you get some rest. We've got some owners coming," he said as he kissed her lightly.

He headed for the door, only to halt and try again. "Because I need to make amends as best I can. Perri—" Matt started to say a great deal more. At the last moment he caught himself. Now wasn't the time. Those oddly colored eyes had revealed too much of her soul.

"Don't get all worked up over it, hon," she said lightly. "I may love you and I may forgive you, but I don't expect to hear of love being returned. And my loving you does not mean I want to be around you right now. So go," she commanded, waving him off. "And let me work through this headache."

Matt smiled, grateful she understood him so well; and sorry that there was need for it. He wanted to say more. But he just couldn't. He couldn't explain how it all weighed on him. The obligation to feel something, in the midst of such upheaval, could bring him to his knees if he let it.

Then there was the hollow knowledge that Perri was better acquainted with—and more a part of the life of—his own grand-father than he was. He couldn't even begin to explain to himself why that hurt so. "Are you saying I didn't get the job done on your headache, darlin'?" he inquired with a lightness that belied his feelings.

"Oh, I don't know, *darlin'*. I'm in your bed, aren't I?" she asked just as lightly.

For an instant he studied her. The rumpled blouse he'd un-buttoned and left on the bed, her lacy bra exposing honey-colored skin and her hand clutching an old locket as if it held the truth. "You're where you've always belonged, Perri," he replied. "And where I need you to be."

"I wouldn't go up there, if I were you," Donnie called out when Matt entered Gledhill and made his way toward the stairs.

He couldn't hear that tone as anything other than a challenge. Probably, because it was just that. "Oh?" he inquired, studying her from the doorway of the dining room.

Donnie never looked up from her scrutiny of Gannie's tapes. "She's on the phone with her father," she said on a sigh. "Trying to convince him how wonderful it is that he's going to be a grandpa.

"Allowing as how you're the daddy, Uncle Mike is being just a bit of a hard sell," she reported. "My advice is to stay down here where he can't reach through that phone and rip your lungs out."

Matt had the grace to wince. "Good point," he answered.

Donnie took some pity on him, but not much. It wouldn't do to go soft now. Honor was at stake. "It will be okay, Matthew," she replied. "It won't take Mike Stone long to remember he has too much hard pride to land himself in jail over a Ransom."

Curious, Matt entered the room. "What are you looking for?" he asked.

"Gallahers," she replied. Donnie turned back to study the wall. "They're out of order."

"Figures. Well, I'll leave you to it," he answered impatiently as he started for the stairs. "Don't worry," he added as sharp blue eyes whipped over him. "I'll tread lightly."

A tiny smile played upon that Kewpie-doll mouth. "You would want to, Ransom," she said, her attention divided between Matt and the tapes. "I enjoyed telling Perri what a low profile you kept in the waiting room today while she was having her exam."

His face hardened into sharp, unforgiving angles. "You've heard already? They're talking about her?" He looked around as if the offenders were present.

"No. Not like they did, anyway." Donnie considered his puzzled expression and judged now to be the time to elaborate. "Not like they did twelve years ago," she said, "when she left so unexpectedly for Raleigh and everyone assumed she must be pregnant." She saw that start to sink in. "Since no one knew about you," she added, "Gannie and Janie were able to nip that kind of talk in the bud."

Donnie made him wait, just a bit, as she moved casually along to inspect a different section of the shelves. "You may not remember how it was, since you were so busy getting yourself married. Here we go," Donnie exclaimed cheerfully as she snagged a set of tapes. "Okay, I'm out of here."

"Perri, I'll call," she shouted up the stairs, receiving an answering goodbye. Donnie then halted as Matt blocked her exit.

They knew each other too well. The dance was not quite done. "No, she's not today's hot topic, mister. You are. What *did* you say to Mrs. Sullivan?" she demanded, poking him in the chest.

"Not nearly enough, apparently," Matt muttered as Donnie hit the screen door and he headed up the stairs.

Matt took in the sight of Perri in the middle of their bed. Then his eyes rested on the book she was looking through. He winced. The title read *Labor: A Contest of Courage.*

"Your headache must be gone," he observed in a dry tone. "What is that about anyway?" he demanded. "Birth among the Amazons?" The green in his eyes reflected the color his face had turned just glancing at the title.

"Donnie brought it," Perri smiled as she sorted through some pamphlets the doctor had pushed on her earlier in the day. "She said it was all over town that you sat in the waiting room discussing babies with Mrs. Christian. Or was it Mrs. Sullivan?" she muttered. "I was too horrified to give my full attention to the details. I'm resigned to the fact that by now they've heard about this baby all the way to the Panhandle."

"It was Mrs. Sullivan, not Mrs. Christian," he answered as he carefully studied her for signs of fatigue. "Mrs. Christian stopped speaking to me when I was still in high school."

"What's this?" A gift-wrapped package rested on top of the chest he had claimed for himself.

"Your wedding present," she answered a little uncertainly. "It was finally ready. Donnie picked it up for me. I was sort of unprepared on our wedding day, Matt. It never occurred to me you would give me something," she said as she used a pamphlet to mark her place in the book. Perri didn't see Matt flinch at her words. "I apologize for that. Do you like it?" she inquired hopefully as he worked his way through paper and ribbon.

He lifted out a memory box. Bits and pieces of hope were encased under glass. Matt never noticed that the hunter-green background and the display case of dark wood nearly matched his eyes. All he noticed was how intimately she knew him, to have created such a gift. All he could see were chips and moments of a life centered around the land.

Turquoise gleamed in a shard of Cherokee inlay pottery, next to a single spur that had once belonged to the first Matthew Ransom. Gannie's little "lady" knife rested near a battered brass matchbox and a French coin from the turn of the century. Each item, each treasure was something the young Matt had found at Gledhill. All represented a time before his pride had distorted his perceptions.

The center of the box held a photograph of Gannie and Matt out back by the old barn. In the background, Ransom land stretched past the fence separating it from Gledhill. He'd never seen the photograph before.

"You took this just before we broke up," he said, his voice husky. Neither of them chose to dwell on the fact that "break up" didn't quite describe what had actually happened between them.

"Just before," she replied on a slow, shaky breath. "I don't have anything else for you, Matt. You don't need another cell phone. You never use your fancy pocket organizer, and I can't afford to buy you a horse. I was unprepared for diamonds and emeralds," Perri added, "and I can't compete with that anyway. So, you only get something you've never known you didn't have. Those are just little bits of things that once meant something to you. Everything else is yours by right anyway."

Her honesty and ease nearly destroyed him. He vowed in that moment to use the memory box not just as a container for mementos of a less-complicated time. He would cherish it as a reminder to keep things simple in the present. Carefully, he stood the box upon the chest and against the wall. Turning, he moved to the bed to sit beside her.

"Thank you," he said, holding her close and breathing in the scent of her hair. They sat wrapped in the silence for long moments. "If your father decides to come out here from Raleigh and shoot me, please see that I'm buried with it."

Perri laughed happily and hugged him back. "Thank you for giving me back something that was missing," he said humbly.

Matt lightly kissed her brow, slowly running his hot, callused palm up her shin to her knee, then up the back of her thigh. It was a while before he finally spoke. "I'm so sorry for my behavior that night." He didn't have to clarify which night he was talking about.

Knowing he meant it allowed her to let go of some of the pain. The events of that night had forever changed him as much as they had changed her. Perri understood that young Matt Ransom would have been honor bound to believe his mother. Just as this man was now honor bound to stay with the land; to make the best with her, because of the baby.

The heat of him scorched her as she nestled in his arms. His hand all but burned her thigh. "It's all in the past, Matt," she said. "We were both so young." Perri smiled at the thought of just how young they had been. "Actually, I'm—"

"I know," he interrupted, "I changed your life for the better. Thanks to me, you got out—you saw more of the world." Matt abruptly cupped her shoulders. "But I hurt you. I was intentionally cruel," he declared. The breath was freezing in his chest. He didn't permit her to disengage from the embrace.

She could feel the relief he didn't try to disguise when she quit struggling. Tenderness seemed so difficult for him now. It had, at one time, been so natural. Now Matt could touch the softer emotions only briefly. For now, it was enough.

Perri could read the desire and intent in his eyes and her body ached for him. They had been sleeping alone for too long. He looked like a man who felt he had every right to the woman lying on his bed. She reached up to smooth his cheek.

Matt's hands slowly moved down her arms. He then took the reading material from her and carefully stowed everything on the floor by the nightstand. He turned off the lamp by the bed and reached for her.

Slowly he rubbed a callused thumb over the satiny skin of her inner wrist, feeling the vein throb as her pulse rapidly accelerated. He seemed intent on absorbing the life energy so apparent within the baby-smooth skin.

Carefully, watching her all the while, he brought her wrist to his lips. His teeth nibbled briefly before she felt his tongue lazily stroke her skin in an openmouthed kiss. Matt's mouth had always been a dilemma for her. It was too full and sweet; too dangerous in a face of such hard angles. He used it now to devastating effect, rubbing his lips and tongue over her. He tasted her skin, inhaled her scent, as her pulse hastened enough to curl her toward him.

She could smell sunshine and wind on him. The blood was moving heavily through her, as she struggled to breathe. Perri felt grateful she was sitting down. He made her too weak to fight the slow, burning sensations that pierced through her.

His dark eyes finally lifted to hers. "Will you let me love you, Perri?" Matt rubbed her other wrist against the hollow under one razor-sharp cheekbone. It sent sparks all the way to her center. "Will you stay with me?" he asked softly, reading the answer in her eyes.

Skillful hands moved to deal with her silky floor-length dress. Slowly he unbuttoned each button, skimming his fingers over each newly revealed part of her. He gathered the bottom of the baggy dress, pulling the full skirt up in bunches to trap her wrists in the satiny fabric. Smiling, his mouth moved back and forth between her exposed breasts, bringing each nipple to a hard, achy pearl. "Will you let me fill you?" he asked in a husky voice.

Matt took the way her body arched as her reply and began a deliberate exploration of her mouth with his tongue. His hands released her wrists in order to slowly tease her panties down her legs. Then a big, warm palm claimed her stomach.

Matt paused to study her. He seemed determined to memorize her body; tracing her belly as if to track each change the baby would soon bring about. Long, callused fingers moved down between her open thighs to linger inside her wet, velvet folds.

Her broken, honest little moan was all the reminder he needed that the day had been one for making repairs. Matt teased and stroked her until Perri writhed in the sensual embrace.

When he withdrew from the kiss and from her body to press moistened fingers to his own lips, she could only moan in protest. Perri moved restlessly beneath him, frantic to unbutton his jeans. "Yes, Matt, please fill me," she pleaded. "I feel so empty."

Those were the words he'd been waiting to hear.

It had rained during the night. *Sultry and sweet,* was his first thought upon waking to the light of early morning. The thought applied to both the morning and the woman, he reflected sleepily. Eyes still closed, Matt's hand moved over Perri as he curled her closer to him. She loved him, he thought, his lips lingering at the back of her neck.

Still asleep, Perri arched her hips into him ever so slightly. The movement was enough. Matt gently moved her onto her back and rubbed his stubbled cheek over her breasts, his straining erection stabbing against her thigh.

Half asleep, half awake, Perri reached for him on a moan of blatant desire. Deeply touched that she would want him even in her sleep, Matt found her hot, wet and as ready as he. Smiling, his mouth conquered one budding nipple, then the other.

He acknowledged a longing, a thought, a hope as sweet as the morning. He vowed to work to turn the present, founded upon mutual duty and physical hunger, into something deeper through what they had shared in the past. *Maybe that would be enough,* he reflected, even if he left his heart out of it. Then further thought became impossible.

The lazy morning mood flashed into one of urgent demand. One moment she was asleep. The next instant, Perri awakened with a desperate need for the man whose clever hands and mouth were teasing her so close to sweet release. Desire rocketed through her. She voiced his name, demanding he settle between her thighs.

Her nails scored his back as he drove into her. Perri cried out, writhing beneath him, instinctively wrapping herself around his waist. A sizzling orgasm had her lifting her hips to take him even deeper.

Matt remained still and contained as long as possible to watch her. To feel her ripple around him. She had never been so daz-

zling, so wanton, so consumed in the pleasure. He held out,
watching her come apart beneath him, until he too lost himself
in the moment. It was hot and fast and hard on both of them.
The heat flared to bursting and beyond before Perri fully opened
her eyes.

They lay still and silent; both aware that he hadn't given her
an opportunity to decline. Both were aware she hadn't wished
for one. Matt finally raised himself up to look at her. The brown
flecks in Perri's eyes glowed like warm honey, making him
smile. He had needed her here, in his bed; needed her for his
soul. "Good morning," he said with a grin. Keeping her with
him, he rolled onto his back.

Unable to let her go, Matt's hand fisted in her hair. It didn't
need voicing that if Perri tried to move away from him, he
wouldn't let her. Deliciously spent and at peace, one broad hand
slowly molded her seemingly boneless body even more closely
to his own.

Perri dug her nails none too gently into his biceps and arched
her back. His laugh was soft with understanding, his hand curving quickly and possesively around her bottom. "You're where
you belong," he stated, touching her intimately. "You're mine.
Say it." Her body responded even as she remained silent. The
lack of immediate reply didn't bother him in the least. It was
only a matter of time.

"You're going to say it, Perri," Matt declared as he continued
to caress her. "You were always mine." His tone gentled as he
remembered how hard he had pushed her, and how fast, to get
her to this moment. And just how much he, too, belonged in her
arms.

He really did want to give her romance, he mused as his other
hand played lightly between her shoulder blades. He just didn't
think he knew how to go about such a thing anymore. And the
woman knew him too well for him to fake it. The thought sobered him slightly.

Matt was willing to learn just about anything, but this wouldn't
come easily. And so for now, emeralds, diamonds and an old
locket would have to do in place of a heart. He steadied himself

in the knowledge that Perri would understand. She loved him. But jewelry wouldn't mean as much to her as an effort of love.

"Hon, we need to get to know each other, don't you think?" he asked. Exasperated, he pulled her head around to where he could look deeply into sleepy eyes. "Will you please say something," he demanded. "Hello?"

She shook her head, trying to catch up. It was just like him; she could register that much. To touch her all the way to her soul, and annoy the daylights out of her at the very same time, was just so typical. How the man expected her to speak, much less think, after bringing her out of sleep in such a devastating manner was beyond her.

"I'm just not a morning person, Ransom," she managed to croak out before dropping her forehead onto his chest. His answering chuckle rumbled hatefully against her poor, unusable brains.

"Okay, sweetheart," he answered in reply to her groan. "You just lie here and think about our spending some time together. Give some thought to a short trip, a getaway. We need some time," Matt repeated. "Time away." *From the past,* he reflected.

"And I need time to look at you," he said as he gently shifted her to his side. "I need time to tell you how beautiful you are. I haven't told you enough how beautiful I find you." The realization sobered him. "I care for you, Perri." Well, *that* earned him a sleepy, puzzled look. "I haven't told you because I can't tell you more," he qualified. "And you deserve more.

"So think of a place you want to go," he added. "Someplace sort of close. Not Fiji." She smacked lamely at him for that. He ignored her, considering. "Maybe Mexico, somewhere on the Gulf. You let me know what you want to do and we'll take a few days away. Hell, we'll try for a week, okay? Think about it," he repeated as he rolled out of bed to start the day.

Matt turned back to smile at her and paused. She took his breath away. He stood silent and thoughtful over her, the look on his face a possessive one.

"Is that an order?" Perri inquired. Fussy from lack of sleep, she wasn't so out of it not to notice that he hadn't once used the word "honeymoon" to describe the trip. Fiji would be a honeymoon. Something like that would take planning and care. Grumpily, she made an attempt to gather the sheet around her.

Matt knelt on the bed and quickly stopped her hand. He had deliberately kept her up all night, as if sleep brought too much of a separation. As if she could be lured away from him by her dreams. Now he kept her still.

"Don't," he appealed as she began to struggle. "I need to look at you, Perri. I need to know you're real." He traced the line of her back as she rolled over in an effort to cover herself. His hand continued its possessive course over each exposed part of her.

By the time he gathered her to him, she was breathless and shivering once again. Perri surrendered as Matt buried his face in her hair. In that one moment, he made her feel cherished. No one had ever made her feel that way but Matt Ransom.

All the things he couldn't quite say shimmered just out of his reach.

Seven

The rain gauge outside their bedroom window registered a quarter of an inch. Checking the sky, Perri vigorously toweled-dried her hair. The rosy sun had a welcome backdrop of dark clouds. And the warm, moist air offered hope that today, someone would get rain. She quickly headed downstairs to set the sprinklers in the front to working. Clearly, it was an ideal morning to water.

I love him, she thought. Yet why she had mentioned it was beyond her. Revealing to Matt that she still loved him wasn't something Perri had meant to do. She was an idiot to have flat-out said it.

The words had just come out of her and felt right at the time. Maybe it had been the headache talking; but her heart knew it was right. She headed around to the back and uncoiled the hose all the while rerunning the exchange in her mind.

Matt had seemed to need to hear the words. She didn't pause to reflect upon what it would have meant had he seen fit to say them in response. Instead, she continued with the task at hand. The raw, bitter harm of loving a man who didn't love her was a pain she couldn't delve into. For now, such reflection was obviously a waste of time. He was hell-bent on maintaining the notion that loving was beyond his range.

As Perri set about tending the backyard, it occurred to her that there *might* be a chance to make this work. There had to be a way to maintain some dignity if she could look beyond her pride. She knew how to adjust. She'd made a life out of adjusting to whatever "stew" of circumstances she had been served by chance. For after losing Matt Ransom, there had been nothing but chance for Perri Stone.

Make the best, she thought, pausing by the back door to watch some monarch butterflies dance. She couldn't let it matter who did or did not love. For a time this morning, he had been so sweet and loving toward her. She had been awakened needing the feel, the rich taste, the scent and the glorious heat of him. And remembering what they had once had together, she had freely given herself.

But Perri understood it meant nothing just because he had momentarily disarmed her with sweetness. He'd been sweet before. It seemed clear that Matt offered her sweet moments as a substitute for love. In frustration, Perri ran her fingers through her still-wet hair and carried on.

Rotating the sprinklers, she breathed in the day. It was a stunningly beautiful morning, and that lovely smell of sun on damp soil and grass filled her with peace. A day like this made it all worthwhile.

The summer heat of Oklahoma wasn't bothering her all that much. She'd adjusted easily to temperatures of over a hundred degrees. And she surely did not miss the humidity levels of New York City, where summer bounced and writhed right off the concrete.

Perri looked up through the branches of the pecan tree to the second-story windows of the back bedroom. Neither she nor Matt had remembered to shut them last night. It was such a pleasant little room, with a lovely view out the back. She smiled at the sight of lace curtains stirred by the breeze. Now that she shared his bed, the little room needed to be used for something special, to take advantage of the view. Maybe she could make it into her office.

A nursery, of course, she realized. Perri shook her head at the obvious and in the process, noticed that the birdbath was filled with leaves from the pecan trees. She moved automatically to clean it. What had happened to her brains? *Too much, too soon,* she thought as she rinsed it out. She had a house to arrange for a baby, for a little family. A house that, at present, resembled a repository for local history.

Just the other day, Perri had found a foot-long, jeweled hat pin from the turn of the century. It had lived in the vanity of the back bedroom for who knew how long. At least a century old, the hat pin was completely useless. But she couldn't bear to get rid of it. And it was just one example of the kind of things she was discovering in closets and on shelves at every turn.

The immediate, the necessary objects or clothes for daily life weren't all that Gannie had kept close at hand. She had truly kept the past wrapped around her. Perri knew she should call the ladies of the Spirit Valley Historical Society about just such items. They'd be itching to go through the place now that the funeral was decently past.

"Oh my nerves," Perri groaned as she moved to turn off the hose and the sprinklers. The two of them had gone for her doctor's appointment yesterday, so half the county knew all about it by now. And that was a conservative estimate. Matt hadn't even tried to remain discreet.

She had to get the place in order. Neighbors had been remarkably hesitant to drop by, in view of everything that had happened. *Like a funeral, an eccentric will and a hastily arranged wedding,* she thought dryly. All she needed was for the church ladies and the historical society—which she acknowledged were pretty much one and the same—to descend before she got Gledhill ready for guests.

She headed inside for the kitchen. At the sound of the doorbell she kept going, praying it was Donnie and not company. A delivery truck was parked in the drive. *Now what?* Perri wondered as she opened the front door.

"Delivery, ma'am. Sign here, please," the lanky, rawboned kid requested respectfully as he eyed her legs.

"Delivery?" Perri echoed in bewilderment as she studied the

invoice. Pasting on a bright smile, she reached for the phone. *What* had the man done now? When Matt picked up, he barely gave her time to get out a greeting.

"Hey, hon. I was just thinking of you," he said brightly. Overlooking the steel underneath her sputtering, Matt took the Oklahoma City exit for Remington Park Racetrack. "You should have come with me," Matt said. "Maybe next week when I'm running some decent horses, I'll bring you out here. I'd like to show you off."

"More 800 stuff? This time from Maine?" Perri demanded as her eyes followed the deliverymen going about their work. "You called a furniture-maker in Maine?"

"What?" he asked, playing catch-up. "Yeah, that's right. I needed a desk and they had some good-looking leather chairs, so I went ahead," he replied, not realizing he was just digging himself in deeper. "It'll go just fine with some of that stuff stored in the basement. Have you been down there?" he inquired conversationally. "I want to move that antique gun cabinet upstairs. Set my office next to—"

"You didn't think to ask me." It wasn't a question. Perri watched Donnie's car pull on back past the truck.

Matt took a considering breath. "I thought I'd surprise you," he answered. He paused to see if she was buying it.

"Why don't you bring stuff from your place, Matt? Why not just bring your things from home over here? It's a whole lot closer than Maine," she pointed out. "At least it's on this side of the Mississippi."

The silence on the other end of the phone threatened to stretch into next week. He was not ready to commit to their marriage for all his big talk. "Well," Perri said quietly. "I guess that says it." That the man couldn't bring himself to move in items from his own home down the road spoke volumes in her direction.

She ignored the hurt and turned to Donnie as she climbed the steps. "Why aren't you asleep?" she demanded.

"Can't," Donnie replied. "I'm too wired."

"Tell me you have the rest of the day off," Perri said tartly, the green in her eyes blazing.

"I do," Donnie answered, as she hit the front porch. "I'm

working the graveyard shift again tonight." Donnie's eyes asked the next, obvious question.

"Good," Perri retorted. "Let's go see how fast I can order new rugs. If you're up for it, go get the tape measure out of the junk drawer, okay?" Matt's answering protest went unheeded as Perri ignored the idiot on the phone.

Sizing up the situation, Donnie's lips curved into a delighted smile. "Revenge shopping on Matt Ransom's dime? I love that," she replied simply.

"Perri," Matt called, "I didn't mean—"

Too late, bub, she thought. "No problem," she said. "It was a surprise, right, Matt? Well, surprise." Perri turned her attention to the workmen as they entered. "Oh no, that's fine," Perri sang out sweetly. "Just leave everything right here in the foyer. My husband can decide where he thinks this stuff is going to go. Oh, a lamp, too?" she cooed. "How lovely." She turned her attention back to the man now sputtering along somewhere in Oklahoma City.

"You are not the only one who lives here, Matt," she said in a snippy tone. "You are not the only one here with air rights, with rights to the space. You come striding through, arranging things to fit your needs, your preferences, without so much as a thought to sharing space or asking me how I feel about your decisions. And your decisions affect me personally," she informed him. "It's the same as not sharing yourself, Matt." She ignored the workmen moving past her and kept talking.

"What if I don't like the chair, or the new desk?" she demanded. "What about this lamp? Of course, the thing that really gets me," Perri continued, "is you didn't even think to ask for my opinion. Just as you didn't even bother to *ask* me to move into your bed."

The nearest workman's eyes popped at that. She wouldn't blush. She flat-out refused. "I'm beginning to feel as if there is no room for me here unless I'm willing to fit myself around you," she said in lower tones. "And I'm getting steamed about it." It was enough to make a woman want to quit. Give up. Withdraw.

Run away, she realized, taking a breath to slow down. Perri knew she was overreacting. She didn't care about the damn chair. It was probably perfect for him. But why couldn't he have included her? Why not share his plans?

"I don't know *how* to ask!" he protested loudly. The workmen heard that too. "If you don't like it, do something about it! If you hate the chair or the desk or the whole thing, send it all back. Your name is now on the plastic," he reminded her. "Go make a home. Get whatever you want."

Perri could hear the hurt through the line. "What I want is the shared experience of making a home with you, rather than your taking it so totally upon yourself to suit yourself," she explained more softly. She moved out onto the porch with the phone. "Nor do I want you just delegating the whole thing to me."

Smiling at the workmen, Donnie took over. They had had enough entertainment for the day. And besides, Perri was on a roll.

"This was an arranged marriage," Perri reminded him as she turned off the last of the sprinklers. "You're going to have to show some willingness, some consideration, for making it more than a series of independent decisions and deeds. If not, then forget about a future that's not 'covered in dust' as you put it. You will have already buried the present. It's going to start out stale and dry," she warned.

She refrained from tying the garden hose into knots just to annoy him when he came out to water in the evening. That was childish and she'd probably pull a muscle in the process. She coiled it neatly away.

"I hesitate to even use the word, but I'm not working on this relationship by myself," she declared. "I'm not going to be the only one to give, to give way." Perri huffed out a breath and listened to the silence on the other end.

"You're right. I'm sorry. I wasn't thinking about how it might look through your eyes," he said humbly. Matt's smile was almost audible through the phone when he realized he'd rendered her speechless. "Perri?" Matt appealed softly. "Make a home for me. Please."

Perri took the phone from her ear and stared at the blasted thing. Now how did a woman argue with that?

* * *

"You're stewing. You know it," Donnie observed as she walked with Perri out into the parking lot surrounding the shopping mall.

"Well, I've got a legitimate reason to worry about the most efficient way to go about this," Perri added, a little defensively. "I have my very own, personal museum and it needs to be turned into a home. You know we should donate at least half of the furnishings."

"Nothing's easy," Donnie muttered as they crossed the lot.

Perri shot her a look. "You're not helping," she stated. "This is really driving me nuts."

"Look, I don't know how much a woman *should* preserve and honor of something that will never come again," Donnie replied, shifting her package from hand to hand. They had been going over this ground for the last hour. "Personally, I think it's best when we make our own history. But I do agree that anybody who is living inside a museum has a problem on her hands, and not just with all the dust."

"I know," Perri sighed in disgust. "But why do stupid things, like a hundred-year-old hat pin, have to stop me? It aches me to take this on. It's too much."

"You know you're asking the wrong person," Donnie continued. "I never look back. I can't. I don't want to and I don't know how. I don't want a damn memory box where I'm reminded everyday of what is long gone. I know I'm not much help, but I'd rather look to the future," she said lifting the package. "I'd rather focus on how cute this lamp is going to look in the nursery.

"And by the way," Donnie added, as they crossed the broiling parking lot, "while we are on the subject of being driven nuts, tell Matt not to call me every five minutes. Tell him not to page me, and not to bother my dispatcher. I am not having my sleep interrupted so he can grill me on whether or not you've eaten properly today," she declared. "Just tell him I tried to make you eat more and you declined." She steered them toward the right row of cars. "I'm not having it. Now goodbye," she said as she kissed Perri's cheek. "Drive safely."

"You know perfectly well I'll drive just fine," Perri retorted as she took the package from Donnie. They had arrived separately, so Donnie could get right home for a nap.

"Yeah," Donnie agreed, "but now you can tell that maniacal husband of yours not to call me about your driving all by yourself." She stopped in the act of unlocking her car and gave Perri a pitiful look. "We are going to have to break him of this. I'm just not up to it." On that comment, she took off.

Perri sat in the parking lot, trying to focus for the drive home. The car was stuffy and blistering hot. The silence that enveloped her weighed heavily. And yet she was loath to move, loath even to turn on the air conditioner.

Motionless, she absorbed the scalding heat. It was so quiet. Sometimes the quiet in Oklahoma could prove deadly to the soul. Sometimes there was violence in such heat and stillness. She started the engine and the air conditioner before she grew too weak to drive.

Pregnancy was changing her, Perri realized. Normally she always preferred to make decisions alone, without assistance. This time she had needed Donnie's help. It had been a swift shopping expedition; with none of the careful deliberation of a young bride making her first home. Perri had gone for the well-made, the sturdy and the practical. Her eye had searched out the baby-proof and the boot-proof.

As Perri drove out of the parking lot, she went over in her mind what she needed to do. The nursery was obviously up there at the top of the list. The handmade, rockinghorse rug she had found was perfect. It made her smile just to think of it. The soft, sunrise colors of pink and blue against the cream made the cutest nursery rug she had ever seen. She had been exhilarated to find something that perfect. Donnie had insisted on purchasing a carousel lamp that picked up the theme of horses. They had gotten a great deal accomplished in a short time.

Her present spirits lifted as she drove out of the city and back into the country. She could slow down. Perri had recently begun to feel sensitive whenever she was behind the wheel. With her pregnancy, even thirty miles per hour felt too fast to her sometimes.

The sight of the colts and calves suited her mood perfectly.

They never failed to soothe her and touch her with hope. She passed a section where Black Angus grazed in a pasture to the left, with a white Charolais herd on the right.

The road home looked so clean, so fresh and so flat. According to the radio, the rain had moved west over the Washita, between Corn and Cloud Chief. The sun was out, haloed by scarflike clouds. It was going to remain a beautiful day.

Upon her return, Perri had quickly regained her natural and everyday interest in rainfall. She hadn't paid any serious attention to it in years. But now, she found herself observing the sky automatically. The feel of weather, it never left you. Not here on the Plains, anyway. She boosted the air conditioner and turned her thoughts to Spirit Valley and Gannie's project.

She knew they had to focus on fulfilling the terms of Gannie's will for the Donated Land. But no amount of brainstorming had sparked a decent plan for action. Perri wasn't in love with any of the suggestions so far. Nothing they had dreamed up felt right; nothing really fit Gannie's style. Maybe she should consider hiring a consultant. Matt's likely reaction to that idea made her grin.

Matt. The way he had looked on their wedding day was something she would never forget. The harsh, unforgiving angles of his face always kept him from looking cute or too handsome. The broad-shouldered power in the man, and the focus he was capable of at every moment couldn't be tamed by a suit. He had looked compelling and so very much in command, his presence filling every corner of the tiny church.

That was what she should center on, Perri realized. Instead of letting herself be run ragged over the minute details of what to do with hat pins and old memories, she had a new life. She needed to keep sight of what was important now and give her heart to building, not preserving.

Is that what had happened to Gannie? Perri mused. *Had she felt this reluctant pull?* Had she been so disinclined to relegate the past to the past that her life's choices had been stopped by it? Had it weighed as heavily on Gannie as it now weighed upon herself? Perri wondered what had happened.

Had Miss Olivia Gledhill been just as unable to properly dispose of that hat pin and move on? And was that why Gannie

had never married? Because she had fallen into the role of caretaker for Spirit's past? Perri knew where she got her love for
Gledhill. But there had to come a point where you stopped
mourning what was no longer and continued on.

And Perri ought to know. Clearly, at present, there was no
room for her at Gledhill. And that, she realized, was pretty much
her own doing. There was no portion of it that she had truly
made her own. She'd made more of a dent into giving the photographs of the Pioneer Women and the tapes of the 89ers space
than she'd made for herself. *And what would they think?* she
wondered. Women who had helped fell the river of grass?

Crossing the river bridge brought an ache to her heart. So little
water flowed, she could see huge sandbars right in the middle of
the riverbed. What water was flowing freely was the color of red
clay. The soil around the bank was so bright pink, Perri could
see clearly where water had evaporated. *That's all I've seen in
Oklahoma,* she thought grimly, *red water.*

Or had she? Perri's foot found the brake by its own volition.
Suddenly the pink rim of soil linked in her mind's eye with the
sight of blue water. She pulled the car off the road and onto the
shoulder just past the bridge. Quickly, she got out.

As always, the wind welcomed her back into its grasp. The
worries and tasks ahead were almost blown away as strong wind,
strong sun and the boundless Plains assaulted her senses. Nobody
back in New York ever believed it when she described the sensation of land so flat, her gaze took in nothing but sky from her
hipbones straight on out.

Gathering her wits, Perri looked more closely at the riverbed
and frowned. Intuitively, she knew there was an answer here to
at least one of the many questions she had plaguing her. Where
was it?

What was it about that red water? No blue water had been
visible from the airplane upon her return home. Certainly, none
she could remember now. There was no blue water anywhere
but Spirit Lake and that was the deep blue of a man-made lake.
Had she seen clear blue water since returning home? And if so,
where? From the car?

All at once, Perri recalled the sight of an egret by a little pond

on Fort Remount the day of her wedding. She had been so struck
by it, she'd had Donnie pull over. That pond had been as blue
as the sky. And just as clear.

Donnie had mentioned a project out on the post. They were
restoring the native grasses or something. Could that explain why
the pond had been the only blue water Perri had seen since she'd
come home? Was it part of the restoration? If so, they were to
be commended. Questions bombarded her as swiftly as the wind.

Perri stared at the red sandbar and pictured blue water surrounded by the windbreaks listing to the south. Pink soil and
blue sky, and a cloud white encompassed her. The colors pinned
together in her mind like the colors of the rockinghorse rug. A
rug destined one day to be an heirloom.

What had the river looked like a hundred years ago? she wondered. Hadn't the water been blue then? Perri's gaze swept over
the river as she tried to picture it. She could probably find a
description of it among Gannie's tapes of the 89ers. In their
stories.

She turned abruptly and stared across at the railroad bridge
running parallel to where she stood. Breathing deeply, she felt
the past link itself with the present. Her hair whipped past her
face as she studied the tracks and drew comfort from the ever-
present voice of the wind. It was in the voices, of course, in the
stories of the 89ers.

Suddenly, Perri couldn't stop the voices. Nor did she want to.
On how many tapes had she heard them speak of loving this
land; because their children were buried here, their wives and
their husbands, their parents? Family remained here. The voices
that she had listened to, the stories she'd read now came back
on the wind.

Well, why not? Why not make room for the past out on the
lake in a way that wasn't just another dry, boring old museum?
Why not give room to those voices? Why not give others access
to them as well? Why hoard the tapes and transcripts of the past?
Why not put them to use? she wondered.

Perri knew she needed to make room for herself and for her
family at Gledhill. And the 89ers needed a place, a home. Perri
Stone Ransom turned, the sun beating down upon her and the

wind by the river causing her to list a little to the south. She took in the sight of the slow, quiet trickle of a formerly powerful river. And allowed thoughts of restoration, of making a home, to flow through her.

Matt felt the sweat between his shoulder blades dry instantly in the breeze. That was the thing about summer in this part of Oklahoma. There was no humidity. It was a dry heat and hotter than the blazes, but the wind remained unbroken.

He stood in the backyard and studied Gledhill's old barn. The tin roof passed his inspection. Barely. At least it looked sound enough. He ducked inside. It was dark and somewhat cooler away from the burning sun. The barn was hardly what you would describe as well insulated, so heat wasn't trapped inside. He looked around. Bright sunlight filtered through the chinks in the wood like sharp, ragged diamonds. The wind came through on a low whistle.

How old was the barn anyway? He knew it wasn't quite as old as the house. He pushed back the brim of his hat to wipe off some sweat.

Gannie had had the outside of Gledhill painted not long ago; and he knew in his bones it was fine. But if he was going to take care of his family, he would have to see to it that the entire property passed some sort of inspection.

And while he was at it, he made a mental note to arrange for Sam's housekeeper to have her grandson continue tending to the yard work. Weeds needed pulling and the honeysuckle was getting a little ragged-looking. He couldn't maintain things in any way other than a haphazard manner himself. There was no time.

Heading out of the barn, Matt vowed to check everything before the end of the summer. The barn wasn't leaning into the garage or anything. And he hated to think of tearing it down; the stalls might come in handy. But he needed to know that everything on the property was safe. There was a child to consider.

The baby. It wasn't too soon to think about an overnight bag for the hospital and a baby monitor for his office. More 800 numbers. That thought ground him to a halt.

Why couldn't he have told her the reason he hadn't moved

his stuff over from his place? Why hadn't he admitted that he just couldn't bring anything of the past with him into this marriage? With no love to bring, everything in his house on Ransom property seemed tainted by the lack.

But Matt wanted this baby and certainly lusted for his wife. By his lights, that had to count for something, surely.

Our baby, Matt thought with sudden, fierce need. Something he had assumed to be a part of his future had only taken twelve years of hell and sorrow to bring about.

The baby would bind Perri to him, Matt knew. She wouldn't leave again. Even if he couldn't give her the love she deserved, she would stay with him for the child. He didn't want to seem insensitive to that fact.

He understood that his triumph over the baby and his ruthless pushing weren't very romantic. He had hidden that sensation of victory instinctively as best he could. But he hadn't been able to completely hide his feelings the day he had realized she was carrying.

He now vowed to do everything; to do more. More for her than any man who might be able to love Perri could or would do. Maybe he could grab some shred of the ability to love he had once felt and build on it. "Enough," he said firmly, returning his attention to the chores.

We've sure been lucky with our weather, Matt mused as he carried a bucket from the back porch of the house to the vegetable garden. It was a glorious day. The newly mowed grass gave off a familiar scent of summer. The wind was remarkably soft and gentle here on the hill. There were vegetables to gather from the garden. And, thankfully, there were butterflies. Hot, dry summers could affect their food supply, making them scarce.

No unforgiving weather, no tornadoes had come barreling down directly into Spirit. Every one of Mother Nature's destructive impulses had, so far, gone around or over them. There had been just enough hail and lightning to make it interesting. He hunkered down to gather tomatoes.

In that instant, a quail shot right past his nose and out of the patch. She hovered over him, squawking fit to be tied. Five of her young streaked out single-file and under the fence, into the relative safety of the neighboring Ransom pasture.

Matt would have ignored her and continued about his business, only mama did not let up. After a careful scan, his eye found the missing baby. The little one was frozen with fear under a tomato plant. While its mother continued to flap out a distraction, Matt rose and moved off.

As soon as he had removed himself far enough to gain mama's approval, the tone of her squawks changed. The little slowpoke then scooted out and headed under the fence for dear life. The quail hovered over her young all the way, like a low-flying, feathered helicopter.

He could just see Perri hovering and squawking over their child the same way. The image made him laugh out loud as he moved back and quickly gathered tomatoes. He'd spent the day thinking about Perri. It had been hard to concentrate on anything else.

Matt set the bucket of tomatoes to one side and returned to watering the yard. All the while he wondered where his wife was now. She had really gotten to him this morning. Perri had seemed distant in the morning after all the wild loving; distant from the connection they had shared in the night.

He felt a little hurt at that. And yet Matt knew he was being foolish. He was giving her all he had to give. It wasn't enough, not nearly enough to build on, certainly. But it represented his best effort. *She'd said she loved him.* It set his mind at ease, even if his own conduct couldn't.

He stilled, thinking of how she'd looked naked on the rumpled sheets. Matt had needed to look at her. He had needed to look at her breasts and thighs, golden in the morning light. The bed linens had been aqua, he thought unexpectedly.

Last night he hadn't even noticed what color they were. In the light of day, aqua sheets and honeyed skin had affected him deeply. He had held her to him for as long as he could, inhaling her scent in an attempt to somehow wrap her around him for the day separate from her.

Matt would push without much mercy if he had to. It was second nature. He would push to maintain the new, fragile connection; to build a marriage. He'd use sex ruthlessly to bind her to him. He'd use anything to keep Perri close, to keep her here. The trip to the Gulf he wanted them to take ought to help, at least he could hope.

Flowers, Matt thought, suddenly inspired. He would buy her some flowers. That was romantic, wasn't it? The thought caused the whole afternoon to brighten around him.

Maybe they sold some candles at the florist's, too. Matt had never bought a woman a candle in his life. *Flowers should help,* he thought almost as a prayer. Matt turned off the hose and coiled it away. He gave up on the idea of calling a florist immediately when Perri's car pulled up the drive.

An intense, possessive urgency clutched at him as she stopped the car by the front porch. Matt was just about to grill her on why she hadn't called when he was saved from such momentary foolishness. Perri got out and headed into the house without so much as a glance at him. He swore and gathered up the bucket of tomatoes before tracking her down.

Eight

Facedown and half asleep, Donnie grabbed at the phone next to her bed. Missing by a mile, she tried again. Her poor, overworked brain couldn't quite grasp why the ringing was coming through so clearly. It was truly puzzling. She had gone to bed wearing her earplugs for just this reason.

As the phone in her hand made successful contact with her ear, she continued her steady crawl toward consciousness. The moment finally arrived when Donnie realized she did indeed have an earplug still lodged in one ear. It was the ear to which she was now dumbly holding the phone.

Its mate was pushing into her cheek. It didn't hurt or anything, she noted sluggishly. And where was her pillow? She had to either change ears in order to use the technological wonder now clutched in her hand, or she had to remove her remaining earplug. Nothing was easy.

"Will you please say something," Perri demanded through the receiver. "You're making me nervous."

As Perri continued to talk, LaDonna Marlowe got it together. After careful consideration, she rolled over and successfully placed the receiver to her unplugged ear. This caused the earplug residing between her cheek and the mattress to roll under the bed. The annoyed groan that followed this chain of events didn't really qualify as "hello."

"I've been listening to the tapes and reading some of the transcripts and I think this idea will work," Perri continued the conversation as if Donnie had a clue what she was talking about. "So all I need you to do is to sit there and agree with what I've already settled on. Just back me up," she urged. "A few minor decisions are all that need to be resolved. Like the vegetables. How about a squash and cheese casserole?" she asked. "Hello? Say something."

"Please," Donnie whimpered softly. "I just woke up. Don't say the word 'squash' to me, okay?" Something unforgettable, made with squash and a can of mushroom soup, had been brought to Gledhill around the time of Gannie's funeral. No one who'd tasted it had, as yet, fully recovered.

"You're right. It's overdone by this time of year. Sorry." Perri paused thoughtfully. "What about okra?"

"I've never liked you," Donnie muttered. "You are a heartless woman."

"I'm sorry," Perri repeated, contrite. "I never know a good time to call when you're working nights. I woke you, right?"

"Yes," Donnie replied, "and I'm begging. Please, do not start my day speaking of anything green or yellow. Not until after I have had my coffee. I'm too fragile," she said, pawing at her remaining earplug. Donnie, being the fragile sort, only drank coffee she had first boiled to death on the stove.

"It's three p.m., cousin," Perri declared cheerfully. "I regret waking you. But this is war."

That roused Donnie enough for her to sit upright and lose her remaining earplug in the bed linens. "All right, why are you calling me?" she demanded as she searched through the sheets.

"As I said, you and John are invited to a cookout," Perri repeated briskly. "Saturday, I'm pretty sure. I have an idea for using the Donated Land to comply with the terms of the will. I'll run it by you once I've got it all worked out. The only thing I need you to do for Saturday is to make a three-layer pie."

The thought of a rich, gooey three-layer pie, resting on a pie crust loaded with chopped pecans was much easier for Donnie to handle than the notion of squash or okra. "Aren't we a little too mature for that sort of thing?" she asked, mainly for form. There was no way to be too mature for three-layer pie.

"It's not for us. It's for the men," Perri confided. "Strategy."

"Cooking as guerrilla warfare," Donnie mused. "I've always maintained that you only *look* like a nice girl."

"You're too kind," Perri replied graciously. "If you could also hunt up that recipe for caramel-fudge brownies I would be forever in your debt."

"You're heartless. You know that?" Yawning, Donnie paused to consider. "I've always liked that about you."

"I'll have fresh fruit for you, some shortcake if we want it. I guess that means whipped cream," Perri muttered absently. "It seems redundant with the three-layer pie."

"Wait a minute," Donnie interjected cautiously. "Caramel-fudge brownies along with pie is not redundant, but whipped cream for shortcake is? I'm not awake enough for this. I must be missing the finer points. Is all this dessert angst because it's your first dinner party since getting married?" she asked.

"No," Perri huffed. "I think I've figured out what to do with Gannie's project. I'm hoping to sell them on the idea over dessert." She paused. There was no reason to hide her concern from Donnie. "I wish I didn't feel as if my idea had to be perfect," she said. "I feel like I need it all planned out, with every detail in place just to get Matt to so much as listen to me. Back me up like you always do, okay? And come early," she added lamely.

"Sure. Anything for our side," Donnie said on another yawn. "But I think you're going about it wrong. You need some of it to be his idea. Make it good, but leave some obvious room for improvement. Something needs to be improved upon for Matt to complain about," she advised. "Make it something he can make better, something that he can fix."

"I'm so glad I woke you," Perri replied respectfully. "What have you been reading? *Scarlett O'Hara's Guide to Estate Management?*"

"Let's see," Donnie ignored her and retrieved an earplug from among the sheets. She placed it carefully on the nightstand. "The brownie recipe is in the same cookbook as the three-layer pie. And I'm willing to do anything if it will get the father of the year off my back until you give birth," she declared, leaning against the headboard. "He's married to you, you know. *You* are the one he's permitted to torment, not me. I'm just your poor, little old spinster cousin."

"Oh, probably nothing will get him off your back," Perri answered, cheerfully. She turned as Matt strolled into the kitchen, his cell phone to his ear. She smiled at him expectantly.

"Is that Donnie?" he inquired. "Saturday works for John."

"It's Donnie," she replied. "We're on for Saturday," she said into the phone. "Go back to sleep."

Donnie hung up the phone and scrubbed at her eyes. She was awake, sort of. She was upright. That was a plus. Yawning, she gathered up enough steam to work herself to where she could hang over the edge of the bed and grope around for her other earplug. As the blood rushed to her head, the phone shrilled.

She considered ignoring it. She knew she'd sound like she was being hung from her heels if she answered. But it couldn't be helped. She wasn't moving fast enough yet for there to be an alternative. Swearing, Donnie arched her back enough to reach for it. "Well, what?" she demanded.

"It's me," Deepwater announced pleasantly. "Why do you sound like you've just run a mile of bad road?"

Donnie gave out with an exasperated sigh. "At this point, I *am* a mile of bad road," she said. "You know, Johnnie, that patch of land isn't worth all this aggravation."

"No," John replied agreeably, "it's worth just enough to have gotten them inside a church."

She rolled the earplug between her fingers, considering. "Twenty bucks says she talks Matt into the project," Donnie challenged as she hauled herself back in line with the world. "After he kicks and screams awhile, seeing as how it's her idea."

John considered. Betting against would just encourage Donnie to work that much harder for. "You're on, squirt," he said with a grin.

* * *

No one blinked. It's sort of like poker without the deck. And when the truth hit her, Perri almost started. Each of them wanted this to work, she realized, but nobody wanted to cave in too quickly. John wanted this for Gannie. That devil had only bet Donnie the twenty bucks to throw her off. And Matt was just looking for a way to say yes.

The four of them were seated around the kitchen table. The wind had been fierce enough to make dining outdoors unrealistic. A tornado had touched down four miles due west of Spirit Valley. For a time, it had been a toss-up over whether or not to head for the basement.

Even now, the air crackled with electricity. But the storm had passed on over the Red to worry Texas. Donnie had checked in with her dispatcher and learned that the Spirit Valley Fire Department had announced the all clear. No one in Spirit had been injured during the storm's passage. A couple of abandoned railroad cars had been struck, however. Fortunately, they'd toppled on an equally abandoned stretch of track.

And so, as three-layer pie, caramel-fudge brownies and fresh fruit were passed around, gratitude was a part of dessert. They had joined hands and voiced a prayer of thanks that the storm had left unharmed those they held dear. This time.

"So, what kind of a building are you talking about?" Matt asked skeptically.

"Well, I'd like something that won't blow away," Perri joked. "That would be nice."

"Ah," he nodded, "a bunker."

Here was the moment for which he had bided his time. Matt knew that by agreeing to the project he could get what he wanted most: Perri firmly entrenched in life here in Spirit Valley. He could keep her here and occupied. This project could silence her idea of getting a job with some Oklahoma City bank. On the other hand, it was a staggering amount of work. She couldn't do it alone.

"I think it's doable, Matt," she answered firmly, reading his look. "And I think it's worth the effort. This may very well be the only existing record of what happened to some of the 89ers," she declared. "We all know that records were fast and loose before the Territory achieved statehood, that births and deaths weren't always recorded. People lived out their entire lives here with no official record. And we all know that's how some of them wanted it."

"Gannie obtained eyewitness accounts of the Run; plus the stories that were passed on from families who had settled in the townsites," Perri went on. "We have the information and the land to house the center. And some of this stuff is fascinating, simply because it's so human. It just makes me want to cry. There are dozens of stories of hope and striking courage, of prosperity after hard times, and of disaster."

"Perri, you don't know enough about it to realize what you're undertaking," Matt challenged.

"I know enough to realize that this feels right to me," she countered. "Look, all we have to do is hire a company to do the technical stuff and we could set up a center for the voices by the lake."

Perri wasn't aware she'd referred to Gannie's tapes as "the voices." Donnie was. So was John.

"There's plenty of furniture here at Gledhill, plenty of antiques to give any building a period feel," Donnie interjected. She smartly tossed the ball into Ransom's court. "You guys must have some idea about what type of building would be best."

"Why not use what we've got on hand," Perri continued, "and just find a way to synthesize it into something more? Matt, I know that it means pushing a lot of paper, but once it's done, that's it. There is only a finite amount of data," she declared. "And we would be giving something back, restoring our history, if you will. Unless you would want to go further, and try to return the grassland back to the way it was."

"Nobody is going to want to come here to look at some tall-grass," Matt declared. "And besides, what do you know about reseeding the prairie anyway?" he demanded.

"What do I need to know?" Perri shot right back. "A person can't spit in this part of the world without hitting a farmer, a field, or a combine. So, will y'all at least think about it? The stories are important," Perri averred softly. "After all, hasn't the land and its history always been for all of us, the one, lasting motif?"

"*Motif?*" Matt exclaimed indignantly.

"Oh, all right! Theme," she snapped. "Happy now? This is as much your responsibility as it is mine, Ransom. I'd be pleased to hear any suggestions you've got."

Matt looked at her for a time before speaking. "I suggest that you'd be taking on a big project. You won't get it done quickly, Mrs. Ransom. This sounds to me like a long, heavy haul. We all have full-time jobs. None of us here will be able to devote much spare time to this."

"I know that," she countered. "So?" Suddenly, it felt like a showdown.

"So what happens when the baby comes?" he asked softly. Too softly.

"I can work this project and be with the baby a lot easier than I could be with the baby working for a bank, Matt. I can be my own boss this way. And besides," Perri continued, "there's no urgency to get everything up and running. There's no shotgun clause in Gannie's will, now that we're married. I reread it last night. We don't have a due date for getting the project on its feet. I can take my time."

"It's too much for you to do on your own," he declared solidly. "And I'm opposed to your idea of working for an Oklahoma City bank anyway." There, he'd said it. He was relieved to see her accept his objection. "And this archive idea is really a full-time job. You've already got one starting soon that will take up all your time," he pointed out. "It's just too much. What Gannie did took more than years—it took up her whole life."

What remained unsaid was Matt's understandable concern: By focusing on the tapes, Gannie had stayed wedded to the past. And he didn't have to mention that his first wife had miscarried twice.

"Fine," Perri said confidently. He'd found a logical way to fix her idea and make it better. "I know someone we could hire as a curator. Someone who was born here," she added. "She could work with me to set it up and then take over. As co-executors we could agree to hire her," Perri added. "The money is there."

The pause lengthened as they studied each other. "It is a huge undertaking, Matt," she agreed gently. "You're right. But I would think that the baby would keep me going, would keep me inspired to provide this link to the past. Just as I would think your baby would prevent me from becoming too wrapped up in it like Gannie. The baby would see to it I didn't overdo," she said, smiling.

Matt smiled back. His pride once again had him licked. But this time, his pride was in Perri. Something true passed between them.

In that instant, at the sight of his hesitant smile, it no longer troubled Perri that Matt only needed her to be a mother to his child. "So," she said turning another brilliant smile on Deepwater, "what's our first step, legally speaking?"

Unwilling to tip the balance of the moment, Deepwater opted for caution. "Give me time to study the prospectus, darlin'. I'll get back to you," he said as he started to rise, plate in hand. It wouldn't do to side with Perri too soon.

"Not before you tell me what you think, Johnnie," Matt challenged.

John gave the appearance of thoughtful consideration. "I think donating some of Gledhill's antiques to furnish a genealogy center out on the property would make an excellent tax write-off," he said. "And it would fulfill the terms of the will regarding the use of that land."

"Write-off?" Matt brightened at that. "Clear this place out at the same time?" A building for the tapes, apart from Gledhill; a container for the past that Perri could get away from, and a project to keep her here all in one neat package. "Sold!" he said.

"It's that simple for you, Matt?" Perri demanded, indignantly.

"There's nothing simple about it, woman," he stated without compunction. "We will be taking a load on our shoulders that is going to weigh a ton. I hope you realize that."

Hiding a smile, Donnie glided silently by to clear the table. No one mentioned the change in pronouns. John and Donnie looked everywhere but at each other as they joined up at the

dishwasher. It didn't take so much as a glance for them to co-
ordinate their next move.

"Darling, do something more than just standing there looking
rough and ready. Stop John and Donnie from loading the dishwasher." Perri huffed as she gathered up her notes.

He wasn't going to let her get away with that prissy tone.
"Well," he said softly as he pulled her toward him, "I am ready,
darling, now that you mention it. And we could try it a little bit
rough. I might like that," he said as he swatted her fanny. Just
as he'd hoped, it annoyed the hell out of her.

Deepwater and Donnie studied the dirty dishes, pretending not
to notice Matt's grin. Together, they made believe that to see
Matt Ransom truly smile at last didn't just ache their eyes.

Nine

Seated at her computer, Perri shivered slightly in the air-conditioning. Outside, the sun was frying everything it touched. She pointed, clicked and waited for a reply from a genealogical resource agency. Then, with happy wonder, she took a moment to study the roses from Matt. The battered silver pitcher captured the sunlight coming in from the dining room window, enhancing their lush colors. Such an unexpected surprise.

Perri sighed with remembered pleasure and lightly stroked a rose. The roses inspired such confidence. They ranged from pure white to blazing red, with some astonishing hybrids intermingled among the solids. She'd been floored when he'd walked in the door with them. It was almost like having the old Matt back, she thought, tapping the locket around her neck for luck.

Thinking of Matt made her smile and dream. Presently, she felt a repeated thump against her sternum. Her finger had continued its idle drumming without her realizing. She stopped fidgeting and clicked to print the open document on her monitor.

Perri was well aware that this search should have been done before her dinner party. She could have presented Matt, John and

Donnie with solid proof that her idea was on target. But she had never gotten around to it.

Here she was, with this idea for the land and the tapes that felt so right; yet only now was Perri thinking about the possibilities of on-line genealogy links and CD-ROM. She was only now learning the difference in an Ahnentafel and an Ancestor File. She could have searched out the possibilities for registering their data in time for the dinner party, at least. *So why didn't I?* she wondered.

She didn't have to wait long for a soundless voice somewhere inside to answer. She had been waiting for approval. Perri held onto the sides of her chair and stretched out her back, the wood cool and smooth under her hands. She hadn't fought for this project, she acknowledged, because it meant too much to her. She had waited for everyone else's approval. She had held back to allow *them* to accept or decline what she wanted to do with the Donated Land.

Who was she kidding? She had waited for *Matt* to decide her idea was all right. Had she fought passionately for her project, it would have hurt too much if he hadn't agreed. If she had committed herself and lost, it would have been devastating. It was difficult to admit that fear of rejection, Matt's rejection, had kept her from doing the necessary research for an idea she believed in. But it was the truth. She had been afraid to put her heart on the line.

Perri swore silently, dismayed at her actions. Such passivity had shaped her past and was reaching ahead, grasping hold of her future. Once before, she had lost it all without a battle. She had given up her home rather than fight back the night Leila Ransom had come to Gledhill.

Worse, she hadn't fought for Matt. Perri had locked away the love she had felt for him and permitted herself to be run out of town. She slumped against the dining room chair as she considered ways she could have acted differently.

Recollection brought rage, chagrin, and remorse welling up inside her. She had accepted Leila's ultimatum without a fight. She'd gone from Spirit Valley, and from Matt, instead of standing firm.

What if a battle would have been unnecessary? Or what if she could have won? Dammit, she had never paused to think it through. A seventeen-year-old girl wasn't prepared to make such decisions alone.

She'd never once considered an alternative way to respond. A dreadful hurt had clouded her logic, her common sense and her choices. Her mother could have, and most certainly would have handled the situation, had she but known. Gannie would have cleaned Leila's clock had she learned the truth. And Gannie could have persuaded Matt to at least listen to reason.

Perri closed her eyes, looking inward for some answers. Raleigh had continued the pattern. She had waited with a plaintive, defeated patience until she had sensed her stepmother's love and acceptance to be genuine. Only then had she relaxed with her father's second family.

Being a lady had meant waiting for approval and never battling back. Now however, as her eye followed the lively curl of a red and white rose, the worst truth she faced was that she had never fought for Matt. She had never fought for her home, or for the life and the family they had planned to make together. She had simply departed, never taking a stand for the man she loved.

It was hardly shocking to note that she hadn't put her heart on the line for Gannie's tapes. It was no real surprise to discover that she'd contained her enthusiasm for the project until the support and approval had appeared in Matt's eyes. Then she had felt secure enough to get to work. But initially she had never said the words "I want."

Perri stared hard at the roses, as if they held an answer. How much more reassurance did she require for it to finally sink in? She was indeed accepted.

How much longer was she going to wait to move into her own life and her role as Matt's wife? Perri sighed. If she was waiting for him to fall in love with her, she was out of her mind.

Okay. Maybe it was time to stand for something that meant a great deal to her. It was no joy to go through life permitting oneself to be so easily dismissed. There had to be a way to use that ladylike patience to change such an unproductive habit.

Perri drank in the sight of roses reflected off the shiny surface of her dining room table. Somewhat reassured, she turned her attention back to her computer screen, pointed and clicked. While waiting for the words "Document: Done" to appear, she stroked her locket and formed a plan to bring about something she longed to achieve. Something for Matt, for her child's future and for herself.

Matt pulled the key from the ignition and idly rubbed his knee. He was dusty, hot and tired. He was also hungry, sleep-deprived and in pain. He'd dodged, but the two-year-old had still managed to clip him hard with a kick.

For once, he reflected sourly, Matt Ransom hadn't been quick enough. He had lost a step all day. Now he was just trying to will up enough steam to make it into the kitchen for a cold beer.

Matt sank deeper into the driver's seat and sighed. He'd sure lost a step with Whit today as well, and the realization did nothing to improve his mood. Both of them had dug in their heels over Whit's self-imposed exile. Remembering their fight over the phone was bringing his headache back.

Yet in all fairness, Matt couldn't accurately qualify their conversation as a fight. Whit didn't fight. He remained amiable, soft-spoken and unbending. You could talk yourself hoarse and Whitaker Ransom would let you.

Matt knew he could work smarter and have the time to focus on improvements if Whit would just come home. But instead, his stubborn little brother wouldn't budge from the Panhandle, where rain was but a memory. He hadn't even made it down for Matt and Perri's wedding.

And Whit refused to voice his reasons. He had changed so dramatically after Matt had married Cadie. Matt had had too much to deal with at the time to remember clearly what had happened to change Whit. If he ever knew.

"Sell out and come home," he'd said. "I need you. You can move into my old place." Matt had pushed as hard as he dared. "Your family needs you."

Whit had remained genial and unmoved by the unexpected appeal in Matt's voice. "That's what coming home would mean, big brother." He had sounded as dry as the land blowing out from under him. "Out here this close to hell," he'd replied, "I don't have to fill your boots."

But that wasn't what was really eating deep. Matt knew what was bothering him most. Perri. He'd been stewing over her all day and it had thrown him off but good. Rubbing weary eyes, for the hundredth time he told himself not to be superstitious over a nightmare and a pregnant wife. It was ridiculous that, even now, such a lousy dream could leave him feeling so cold inside. Matt wasn't the sort to ever heed a dream.

He had jolted awake in the middle of the night, frozen with the hypervigilance of the hunted. Matt had lain beside her holding his breath, trying to capture the source of such acute fear. In the dream fragments that had remained upon awakening, Perri had been lost to him. He could vividly recall trying to get to her. He'd been desperate to keep her safe; yet, there'd been no sense of any specific danger. But every effort, every move he had made to reach her in the dream had been performed in agonizing slow motion.

In an unfamiliar room of an abandoned shack, Matt had felt a heavy weight bearing down on him. Heart pounding, he had made a determined effort, but it was as if he were moving underwater. He had fought the hindrance with a recklessness born from the unspoken knowledge that he couldn't get to Perri because he was so lost without her.

His efforts had finally landed him at the front door, which he had wrenched open. The countryside beyond the old shack had been a disturbing sight. Matt had recognized bayou country; however, the dream landscape had been completely frozen over. He was a man unaccustomed to ever being so out of tune with his environment. And yet he had surely been at odds with the dreamworld before him. The open door led out onto an eerie landing and on into a swamp. But no bateau or pirogue could ride through that.

A fog of suspended sleet had swirled over a stream of solid ice. Curtains of icy Spanish moss had cascaded from the oaks. A frozen bird, perching on a smooth, frosted stone, had looked as if it would burn cold to the touch. And a green snake, its scales glistening with ice crystals, had curled comfortably on the landing.

The iced-over swamp had been such a terrifying sight he'd jolted awake. Sweating and needing reassurance, he had waited for dawn, with his hand gently resting on Perri's hair. Grounded by her scent and the sound of her even breathing, he'd desperately searched inward to pin down the danger.

The lush scent of honeysuckle, mingled with a mild undertone of alfalfa and horse, returned him to the present. Matt made the startling realization that he had gotten out of his pickup and was trudging toward Gledhill's glass-enclosed back porch. He'd done it all on automatic. "I really am out of it," he muttered on a yawn. He promised himself a beer and a shower. Hell, he'd just take a beer into the shower, he figured, as he opened the back door and entered.

"What the hell are you doing?" he demanded, shoving his hat back from his forehead.

Twelve floor-to-ceiling windows made up the enclosed back porch. Taking in the chaos, he noted that Perri had pulled all the furniture into the middle of the room. Armed with plenty of rags and window cleaner, she was at work on an east window.

Perri looked up from her efforts and frowned. "What happened? Why are you limping?" she demanded, her voice sharp with concern.

He knew she lived in apprehension of the ordinary accidents that went along with his job. "My knee. I got kicked. Tell me we have cold beer," he commanded. Matt slammed down on a residue of alarm and never registered the tiny coil of anger that swiftly twisted to life. He flicked on the ceiling fan, a little belatedly he reckoned, and considered turning on the air conditioner as well. "You shouldn't be working like this, Perri," he declared. "Not while you're pregnant." Even he didn't care for his overbearing tone, but too bad.

"We have beer," she replied, sticking to what she obviously considered to be the essentials. "I'll get you one, along with an ice pack."

"I don't want an ice pack, dammit, I want a beer," he grumbled as he hung his hat on a peg. She was not going to distract him with that ice pack.

Matt's fury mounted as he followed her. He looked around the kitchen, letting his eyes linger over each familiar object. He made a genuine effort to ground himself in the mundane, everyday signs of his life. But it didn't happen. The kitchen felt alien, as unreal as the room he had tried to escape last night in his dream.

He was overreacting due to fatigue and pain and he knew it. But for some reason he couldn't quite nail down, it set him off to see her engaged in everyday domestic activities. She tossed him a beer as he limped into the kitchen.

"At least sit down and rest that knee while you eat something. You look beat," she said gently.

"I'll shower first," he declared, turning toward the hall. He wasn't doing it solely to be ornery. He really needed a shower. "I won't be a minute." He didn't need it pointed out to him that he was about done in. Taking a sip, he puzzled briefly over his own contrariness as he started for the stairs.

A shower and clean clothes didn't improve his mood. "You've been a busy girl today, haven't you?" Matt asked as he reentered the kitchen and sat at the table.

The economy of movement and the efficient way she'd quickly gotten food to the table during his shower touched the same raw nerve that had been pressed hard in his dream. He still wanted to get to her. However, being awake seemed to have soured the dream's desperate need. Matt couldn't seem to help himself. He wasn't proud of the fact that pain could make him mean. He ignored the ice pack she placed before him. "What did you do today besides move all the furniture and inhale cleaning fumes?" he asked, hoping to lighten the mood.

Perri sighed and brought the potato salad to the table. She had promised herself that today she would take action. She had promised herself that this time she wouldn't wait patiently, hoping for her turn. And a promise was a promise. "Well, I did some thinking about our trip," she replied. "I've decided where I want to go."

Matt looked at her expectantly. She smiled in spite of the nerves. Why was making a clean request so very scary? Probably because Matt Ransom was sitting there in such a stormy mood. "Here's what I think will work," she began. "While the house is being painted, and the carpets are being installed, we can take our trip. Donnie said she'd oversee things while we're gone."

"Corpus?" Matt asked with a nod of thanks as she passed him the sliced tomatoes. Warm water would help his knee. Maybe he'd soak in the hot tub later tonight. Maybe Perri would come in with him. The evening's possibilities suddenly looked brighter.

"No, not Corpus Christi," she replied. "What I'd really like is to go to San Francisco." Perri smiled at the puzzled expression on his face. "I want to feel cold, Matt. I want a break from this heat. And I'd like to be in a city. You know, urban impact and all that. And I need to smell the ocean," she added.

"There's a little hotel in Chinatown with the most amazing domed rotunda in the lobby. Stained glass windows depict the settling of San Francisco," she continued as she watched him build a sandwich. "It's not at all fancy, but the management is very gracious. Of course, you may prefer something bigger and newer. That would be okay with me, too," she added breathlessly. "I don't care so much where we stay. But I'd like to visit San Francisco."

"Okay," Matt agreed easily. "You don't have to sell me on it. That's fine. Cool weather sounds good to me, too," he said. "It would be a pleasant change not to have the wind dry the shirt on my back just as fast as I can sweat it out." He would ignore the import of that word, "cold." There was no reason to consider it significant. It had just been a bad dream, that was all.

Perri took a deep breath and sipped from her glass. "And on the way back, I'd like to stop in Tucson to see my grandmother and your grandfather." She watched helplessly as he mentally distanced himself from her. "I called them," she added. "Grandma Anne and Larry are staying put this summer and said 'Come on.'"

It all came out in an awkward surge of words. "I'd really like to spend a day or two visiting," Perri went on. "We don't have to stay with them. We can stay elsewhere,'' she added quickly. All the need, all the longing flew out of her like a runaway train down a straight line of track.

"No,'' he said, carefully placing his sandwich back on his plate. It was too much. The bones in Matt's face were set, frozen hard and unrelenting around that one word.

"Why not?'' she asked. "I'd prefer to go now rather than travel later when I'm closer to term. They are, after all, our grandparents. They're our family—''

"They're not my family,'' he interrupted bluntly. "They're yours.'' Matt sat perfectly still as the cold spread through him, freezing everything. Even time seemed locked in ice. "My father and my brother are my only family,'' he declared as his vision turned inward. He could almost smell the destructive scent of misplaced pride riding on his words, but he couldn't stop them.

Perri blinked in shock. She'd risked a great deal by simply making the request. She'd exposed a private longing to repair the rift between their families. And he'd willfully slammed her down. She couldn't help but notice that she hadn't been included in his "family.'' So much for how Matt always thought of her as "family and home.'' He'd just made a lie out of his own words. And those words had given her such hope.

In a detached, absent manner Matt observed his own dulled wits. He was too sleep-deprived to know if he really meant what he was saying. It was all too much right now. But that didn't stop him from making it worse. He rubbed his stubbled jaw. "Do you think you could maybe have a little patience, maybe slow down a little?'' he asked, surprised to hear himself say such a thing.

"Patience?'' she echoed carefully. If he hadn't just hurt her feelings so badly, she would have laughed out loud. Matt Ransom didn't know the meaning of the word.

"Look, I'm trying,'' he declared. "Give me time.'' The hurt in Perri was tangible. It was clear that his words were shattering to her. Guilt rose up like a cloud of dust and curled into defensiveness so quickly he didn't even record its presence. He rode right over the knowledge that he was being unreasonable. "Don't push me, okay? It's too soon.''

Well, that did it. Her temper flared to life. "Too soon?" she repeated. "With the way you've pushed me right from the giddyap? You've demanded and demanded from me since the day the will was read," she pointed out. "And I've taken it for the sake of peace. You've made changes in this house almost daily without including me in your decisions. But it's too soon for *you* to make an adjustment?"

She was livid. Perri grabbed the ice pack she'd brought to the table as a tangible reminder to cool down. She never got this angry; it didn't pay. But this time, she wouldn't back off.

"This isn't easy, dammit!" he erupted. "I have tried."

"Yes," she agreed, praying for patience. "It was sweet and thoughtful of you to bring me the roses, but that—"

"I have tried!" Matt repeated. "I sure as hell was not prepared for our having to get married to protect this place. Or for you to get pregnant. It's tough enough for me to adjust to being married again," he declared recklessly. "Real tough, especially since the marriage was to you." As soon as the words were out of his mouth, Matt wished them back.

There was a dangerous silence. "Tough for *you* to be married again to *me*," she echoed with dangerous calm.

"You left!" he exploded, pounding his beer down so hard the silverware trembled. "You took the easy way out and ran!"

She had run from his mother's poisonous lies, not from him; he knew that. To bring it up at this moment caused Leila's presence to all but shimmer in the air. He could almost see her cold green eyes glitter with pleasure at his outburst.

"I took the easy way out?" she echoed. "How about the courage it took to leave Spirit Valley, Matt?" she demanded. "To leave my home in order to protect my mother's reputation? How about what it took *not* to stay in a world where I was no longer wanted? It took everything I had to remain silent about what Leila was doing and let you peacefully get on with your life."

Perri rose, deeply offended and not about to let him off the hook. Everything she had ever refrained from voicing came pouring forth. "Do you think it was easy not to fall apart when you got married so damn fast?" Her voice was low and raw. "Such speed was just a bit indecent, if you want my opinion. How do you think I felt when I learned someone else was having your baby?'' she demanded, her voice breaking. ''You think that was easy for a seventeen-year-old girl who loved you? You tossed me aside as if I meant nothing to you.

''Just because I learned to make a life of my own, acquiring some new skills while I was at it, you think that was easy? Easy, comfortable and safe, right?'' Perri realized she still held the ice pack, squeezed so tightly in her hand it was ready to pop.

''You left, dammit!'' Forgetting his throbbing knee, Matt sprang from the chair. Suddenly that was the most important thing in his world. It had shaped him and he had never examined what it had meant at the time.

''*You* let me go!'' she answered. ''You don't know enough about what I've been through to tell me I took the easy road, Matt,'' she said with quiet rage. ''You never once asked what it was like for me. You never once expressed an interest in how I managed to go on. And while you talk about your struggle to adjust to being married again and a father,'' she added, ''try to remember that I'm not the one who held the gun to your head!'' The ice pack miraculously landed in the kitchen sink instead of right between his sorry eyes.

Bewildered at his own volatile behavior, Matt thought before he spoke. He was unprepared to discover that there might be any fragile, compassionate places left in him. He had assumed for some time that he no longer harbored any feelings of love or tenderness. Matt's anger turned inward as he rested an arm on the old refrigerator.

He just couldn't face his grandfather. And he couldn't explain why. Not yet. he understood that his intemperate position was Leila's work. She had schooled him never to forgive long before the night he had broken up with Perri. But it hurt him too much to face the extent to which his mother had tainted his thinking for her own purposes. It was too soon for Matt to face his grandfather and Anne Marlowe Ransom. Waves of cold fury rolled over him. He waited, silent and stiff, for the right words to express his feelings. Matt waited a very long time. Nothing came to mind.

"Well," Perri said finally. "I guess that makes it crystal clear. So much for your considering me a part of your family." And so much for stating her own needs.

"Perri—"

She held up a palm to halt the discord. "Please. I don't know how we got onto this. I just wanted to go to Tucson. But since we're on it," she continued, "I might as well admit that I made a huge mistake back then. I never defended myself. I walked away, and it changed my life. *You* changed my life," she said, "and in a very real sense made me who I am today."

"*I* made you into someone who has 'taken' my demands 'for the sake of peace'?" he inquired sarcastically. "The poor little victim of all my decisions? The hot little broodmare of 'dubious bloodlines'?" he asked, throwing her words back at her. "Unloved and knocked up? That's the person I've made you today?" he demanded. Now was not a good time for her to touch his heart.

The fight had gone too far. All the pain and loss flooded into a heart that was breaking. "I've changed, Matt," she declared firmly. "Not everyone can say that." Perri fought through the deep sense of hurt. "I know I'm worth more than the treatment I received from you back then. And I'm worth more than this."

Tears settled in as Perri accepted defeat. "Maybe it's best for me to know right now that this is how you feel about it. You don't consider me a part of your family," she said.

Family. The realization slammed him. With the exception of Gannie, Matt had grown accustomed to excluding women from his mental picture of family. The silent discontent of his grandmother, mother and wife had made such an omission possible.

"What difference does it make anyway?" Perri added, when he didn't even bother to dispute the statement. It pained her to say it, but the truth was right in front of her. "There's nothing real about this marriage."

"The baby is real," Matt declared.

"The baby is mine," Perri responded instantly. She was cold and lethal now.

Matt had her blocked at the counter in the next instant. A

sudden, vicious alarm stirred him. "What do you mean by that?" he demanded softly.

She looked at him as if seeing the truth for the first time. The truth about him. "I mean that I'll have a family when I have my baby," she explained. "I'll be part of my own family, Matt."

Desperate, Matt played his ace. "You said you loved me," he reminded her. "You wouldn't have slept with me if you didn't love me."

"And you said nothing," she responded calmly. Too calmly. "From my point of view, that says it all."

"What do you mean?"

"Matt, you couldn't tell me you loved me. You've made a point of never saying it," she replied with such a matter-of-fact tone it sent chills skittering down his spine. "You can't do it now. And you've made it clear. Sam and Whit are your family. I'm not included in that. Please don't misunderstand," she said rigidly. "I can admire your honesty. You've never been less than honest about it. You can't love me."

Well, she had him there. He felt her spirit withdraw as he stared into green and golden eyes filled with tears, courage and pain. He'd hurt her.

"I left once before even though I loved you, remember? So, I love you," she said simply as she moved his arm out of her way. "And you want me for Gannie's land and for the baby." She turned to the table and began tidying up.

"You need me now for the baby," she reminded him. "Without the land and without the child, I'm not valuable to you. Oh, you enjoy the sex, but I'm not someone you're real enthused to have as family," Perri said before she faced him again. "After all, my mother was a Marlowe. My ticket into a family with you is this child." She paused to consider. "It may not matter," she added.

"Stop it!" he demanded. Matt knew there was more to his link with her than that. He just couldn't seem to voice what it was. "You're family. You are my wife," he added, as if it meant something to him. He realized, belatedly, that it did.

"And you've counted all along on my long-standing love for

you," she answered. "You've never bothered to ask, never tried to win me over, whenever you've wanted your own way."

She glanced around but refrained from any more busywork. "You've done just as you pleased," she declared. "And why not? I love you and you know it. You expect my devotion. You don't have to want me for myself."

This wasn't going the way he had planned. *Call her bluff*, he figured. *Buy some time until you can think straight.*

"And do you really want me for myself, Perri?" he asked bitterly. "Because this is it. I'm not some love-struck kid anymore and never will be. Honey," he said, caging her against the counter, "you're lucky you ran when you did. You would have found yourself married at eighteen and terribly disillusioned. It seems to me you haven't changed as much as you'd like to think you have.

"Not that it matters," he went on, echoing her words. "None of that changes the fact that this is all the marriage you've got and are going to get from me. I raise horses and farm for a living," Matt reminded her. "I don't need a woman to get my heart broken. She'd just have to get in line."

"Agreed," Perri replied. "You don't have the time or the heart."

It suddenly dawned on Matt that he didn't know many happy women, certainly not in his own family. Could he live with himself if he were the reason the life got drained from Perri?

"You aren't a part of this world anymore, Perri" he told her coldly. "You've changed too much. You've been too far away, removed from Spirit for too long. You'd never fit into a family down here." He registered her sharp intake of breath as she tried to turn away from him.

An unexamined longing flared just on the edge of his reason. Had *he* ever wanted to leave Spirit? He had never considered such a thing; never thought of it as an option for himself. Maybe that said something about deeply buried needs of his own. Needs that had remained frozen over; needs he only knew how to fulfill one way.

"You must want Gannie's land even worse than I thought," she replied in a hoarse, hurt voice.

"This is all we need between us," he stated, locking her against the counter with his body. "This is what I need right now." Matt cradled her neck in one broad hand and ravaged her mouth.

She couldn't run. And Matt wasn't going to let her pull away. One small part of her resisted, but the strong arms and strong will of the man holding her carried her deeply into his heat. And the feel and the scent of him seemed so right. In spite of everything, Matt's strength and desire for her created a safe harbor for Perri's own needs. The taste of him flooded through her and she melted into him. He abruptly moved one muscular thigh between her own.

His hand warmed her belly, then moved to the waist of her shorts and swiftly past her damp panties. Instantly she was hot and so very wet. The slow, involuntary grind of her hips made it evident the desire was not one-sided.

As she pressed his hips more closely to the source of her heat, Matt felt such a sense of exultation in his own intense need for her.

"This is real, here and now, hon," he murmured as he rubbed his thumb over her jaw and into her mouth. Perri drew his thumb in deeply, licking and sucking delicately. "We both know I could have you this minute and you couldn't stop me," he whispered as Perri moaned, taking little bites of his thumb. "You'll be staying right here. I'll see to it. You're not taking my baby away from Spirit."

Nothing he could have said would have killed off the wild pleasure he had called forth so easily. Her body froze for a long moment before she pushed him away and quickly righted her clothing. "You're wrong about my not being able to stop you, Matt," Perri declared. "I've just never wanted to. Until now." Her fingers trembled as she removed his locket.

Matt didn't like himself very much at that moment. "Fine," he said. "You have a right to want more from a marriage than I'm able to give."

Didn't she realize this was where she was supposed to say she loved him enough to stay? "When the terms of the will are fulfilled, I'll start divorce proceedings immediately," he said formally. He continued to kill them both with a reasonable tone. "Maybe you would consider giving me custody of the baby." The words were out of his mouth before it registered what he had said.

Speechless with fury, for the longest time she stared at the necklace in her hand. Finally she spoke through a wall of inchoate rage. "If you think I would ever consider giving up my baby, you are truly out of your mind," she assured him. "Just because I've bent to every blasted demand you've made since I got here, don't even think that I would give you custody and fade away." Finally she looked at him, her eyes like emerald fire.

"I want that child raised right here, Perri," he persisted. "I'm not going to permit you to teach our child by example how to run. It goes against everything I believe in."

"Married, or divorced, I'm staying, Matt," she said defiantly. "I won't be 'taking the easy way out.' You won't be able to say that I ran. You've stated your priorities quite clearly. I understand." Her voice sounded raw as she placed the locket on the counter.

"You have the beginnings of a family and you're turning me loose. Turning *us* loose. Very well," she said softly. "Start practicing what you're going to tell our child when he or she is old enough. You will be the one to explain why Daddy lives down the road and on the other side of barbed wire." Suddenly afraid that she sounded like the world's most pathetic little victim, she turned, grabbed her purse and car keys and headed for the door.

"Where are you going?" he demanded. For a man with a bad knee, he could move it when he wanted to.

"Out," she replied, too numb to struggle against his grip on her shoulders.

"Succinct, Mrs. Ransom," he answered, "but I need more information. You're not driving off without a word like my first wife did. Where are you going?" He couldn't help shaking her slightly, not with the way his hands were trembling. The scent of her clung to his fingers. The taste of her still lingered in his mouth.

"To visit my family, Matt," Perri answered hollowly. "I'm just going to Donnie's for a while."

Silently Matt released her. It didn't come easily. The urge to keep her flooded through him. "If you stay in Spirit, you'll have to hurt," he declared, knowing he was speaking for both of them.

"No," she replied with conviction, "I'll live. I'll live without what I've wanted most, but I'll live and teach my child how to love. No one will drive me away again." ·

Matt remained silent and unmoving as he watched her walk. And it killed him. The setting sun, surrounded by popcorn clouds, brought out gold glints in the dark blond hair that swept past her shoulders. It had been much longer the last time she had left him behind, he realized. Who was he kidding? If she'd left him behind before, it was because he'd had a hand in driving her away. He curbed his thoughts. It was best not to remember the last time he and Leila had driven Perri Stone out of town.

Matt stood at the door watching her. And grew increasingly worried. For the longest time, Perri sat in the car, going nowhere in the heat of evening. Finally, much to his relief, she started the engine and headed down the drive.

He felt as if his windpipe had filled with iron filings. Had he really said those things to her? Matt wondered as his gaze followed her progress. Here he was, with the beginnings of the life he'd ached to have. He'd been given a second chance with the very woman he'd always wanted, and he'd just run her off.

Way to go, Ransom, he thought bitterly. Matt was honest enough to admit he had never made any effort to help heal the wounds life had landed on her; on either of them for that matter. He'd been resisting ever again having anyone be that important to him.

And yet, she was having his baby. It wasn't to his credit, but in truth he was afraid to build anything with this woman. Not being able to make it work for real with Perri would hurt too much. It was best not to try.

There wasn't much drama about Perri, as there had been to Leila and Cadie, he noted idly. He took the time to recall how Perri had been an example of grace under pressure ever since her return to Spirit. Matt had silently admired how she'd handled herself. How she'd handled him. He had been wrong to lash out at her. *Too late now,* he thought.

He tracked her car to the front. Why had he made it so that she'd been forced to handle so much? She had complied with his demands for this marriage right from the start. He could have met the woman halfway.

Matt understood how it must look to her. His covert triumph over her pregnancy must have seemed like solid evidence that he didn't love her. Particularly when coupled with the fact that he couldn't say those three, simple words. He had succeeded in binding her to him through her love for him. But he hadn't done a blessed thing to deserve or protect her love.

Pregnant, that would hurt even more. Well, that sudden realization had occurred way too late in the day to do him any good. She'd gone as far as she could go. And now, she'd gone to Donnie's.

It didn't look good for him. Matt had maneuvered, and strategized, and protected his heart. He had managed to isolate himself in the frozen landscape of his feelings, where he truly couldn't get to her. And he'd managed, through his own efforts, to convince the woman he couldn't love her. The truth was, he hadn't tried. Suddenly, Perri's words in response to his own came back to haunt him. "You let me go!" she'd cried. That he had.

Matt watched her car turn east. He grabbed his keys and headed for his pickup. He wouldn't stop her and he wouldn't interfere. But he would see to it that his wife made it safely to the only family he'd led her to think she still had in Spirit Valley.

Ten

Doggone it. The weather had tarnished the silver. Annoyed, Donnie glared at her wrist.

Donnie had just put the phone down from trying Perri. She wasn't really worried to receive no answer. Perri had been grieving but okay the night before, when she'd left Donnie's place for home. After all, fighting with Ransom took a lot of energy. A nap the day after combat was only sensible.

Donnie had been staring at the receiver, as if it could tell her whether to leave another message, when she'd noticed that her wrist had turned gray from her bracelet. That the engraved sterling could be so affected by the impending storm made Donnie smile ironically.

She tried to take in a deep breath. The very air around her now felt dulled and lethal. Donnie rolled the heat and tension from her neck and put whimsical thoughts aside in favor of duty. She would, by necessity, make it an early night. She needed to get going at an indecent hour in the morning in order to swing by the old Marlowe place before work. It was her responsibility to make sure it had survived the coming storm undamaged.

In LaDonna Marlowe's considered opinion, Spirit Valley was one of those places people either left at once, as soon as they could, or they stayed on forever. Donnie had stayed and claimed it as her home.

She felt little personal concern about riding out the approaching tempest. Everything she owned had been secured. After all, everything about Donnie was battened down. There were never any edges to tear loose.

And when her shift started in the morning, she would be ready to serve. She figured to try Perri again in a while, before she started worrying. On her way into the shower, Donnie turned off her brain and prepared herself to deal with the morning. And with the aftermath of damnation.

The spirits over Spirit Valley were restless. It was going to be a savage night. John Deepwater watched the setting sun and the rising moon balance each other in the sky from his observation point on the parapet watchtower of his house in Spirit. *A good night to raise hell,* he mused. It was the perfect night for trouble.

He listened as the wind whipped gracefully through the old, majestic elm in his backyard. What would it be like to give in to the dark side on such a night? To become one with the savage winds, rather than to stand and offer up a civilized resistance?

Well, he wasn't going to find out. He had some deposition digests to wade through. That is, if hell didn't pay him a visit first.

Just then, a noisy wind spiraling through the old elm scolded him. John loved that tree. He loved the sound of it most of all. Sometimes he felt that Gannie had left some part of herself in the old elm. It had her personality.

So. No going with the wild side. He had an obligation to the community, after all. An obligation to stand ready for the morning; for the time when the heatburst had played itself out. He would be there for Spirit, prepared to assist in whatever way would be necessary.

But still, it was a night to dwell on the possibilities in going over the border. A night to speculate on the odds in making it back safely. And on the conscious choice that he had made in turning away from such hazardous shadows.

He took in the view from the watchtower again, and thought of Gannie. Once again he blessed her for pulling him up short and setting him straight. Then John Deepwater began to remove his portable telescope from the parapet. Before it was too late to save it.

The woman could still fill out a pair of jeans, Sam Ransom thought as Janie Stone moved quickly out her front door and toward his car. It pleased him no end to see her running out to greet him. He relaxed a bit as he killed the engine.

Sam had been doing some hard thinking all the way into Oklahoma City. He hadn't even turned on the car radio so he could reconcile in his own mind just what he was going to say. They needed to talk some sense into their children. They had to talk before that fool son of his ruined a second chance for something precious. It wasn't going to come easy. Sam knew he was demanding of Matt what he had never undertaken himself.

The fight they'd had still blistered his soul. Sam had not been best pleased to discover his eldest drinking alone and spending the night on Ransom land.

Remarks had been made by both of them that were meant to be forgotten. For the time being, this was the only road open to him and he was by damn going to take it.

And it had taken everything he had just to pull into Janie's driveway. But it was time. After all, he reasoned with a wicked grin, they were family now. They could unite over the coming baby. That baby had the power to bind them and to heal the wounds. The possibility of a Ransom-Stone baby could make some room for them, surely.

Sam leaned out of his window, intent on sweet-talking a pretty lady into going for a drive. All around him, the night bordered on the wild. Something was in the air; Sam could sense it. But Oklahoma City felt to him as if it would stay out of harm's way. This time.

As Janie came closer, Sam noted she wasn't smiling. There were traces of love and regret in her pretty eyes, as always. But fear and urgency overpowered everything as she reached the driver's side of his car.

"You'd better head on home, Sam," she said with quiet gravity. "It's on the news—there's a heatburst forming over Spirit." Her eyes never left his.

Janie didn't have to spell it out for him. "Get inside and stay there. It may feed on itself and reach this far east. Promise me, Janie," he added sharply, recognizing that look. "Matt will take good care of your girl," he said, turning the key in the ignition and shifting into reverse.

A day without her and he was lonely. It had been a slow, lonesome day anyway; the silent kind with which Matt usually felt most at home. He reminded himself of that as he paused to look around. The very light seemed to change with the horses stabled. The different colors of their coats and the different colors of their individual personalities brought out varying shades of light in the stalls. Matt had stayed busy, letting the horses soothe him.

But he still needed soothing. His knee throbbed and so did his conscience. A fight with Sam; and yet, so much had remained unsaid between them. How he hated to fight with his father, especially over Perri.

The more Sam had tried to talk it through, the more icy and withdrawn Matt had become with each awkward attempt. Neither father nor son was any good at sharing from the heart. Matt's definitive response had gone one toe over the line into cruel. And now he'd kick his own butt for it if he could.

Just because it was true Sam had never gotten himself on a plane to visit his father, that was still no excuse for some of the things Matt had said. Last night, it had boiled down to either getting a little drunk, or maybe coming to blows with his old man. As a result, this evening Sam had gotten into his car and driven off without a word about where he was going. And Matt was aching.

Looking back on it, Matt regretted shutting out his father. But at this point, it was one more regret among many. Regret had built as he'd sat in his pickup in front of Donnie's place the night before. For an hour or so he'd willed himself to knock on the door and get his wife. Matt hadn't done it and the opportunity had passed.

Now as much as he would like to mend this rift with Perri, he couldn't see the point; not in the blazing light of day. All he would do, he was certain, was hurt her again. And he had come as close as he ever wanted to get to breaking her.

He had gone back to Gledhill at around three a.m., intent on raising some hell. Walking in the door as if he owned it, Matt had fully meant to demand his way back into her good graces. But the old house wouldn't let him.

Gledhill had felt so sad to him. Despairing. As John had said: Gannie had wanted them to stake a claim, to "homestead." Matt had felt it. With every step, Gledhill had drained him of his anger and arrogance.

Matt had paused in the hallway, before the formal photograph of Vienna Whitaker and her son. Enough light had seeped in to reveal the severe visage of the first Matthew, and just how much Matt himself resembled this man of unknown stock. *Ransom: The price of redemption; an atonement.* Well, maybe not tonight.

When he'd silently entered their bedroom, moonlight had illuminated the memory box. The box she'd made for him contained such love.

Suddenly, Matt had been flooded with images of the woman Perri had become. Her quiet poise in John's office had come to mind. Perri's willingness to marry him to ensure the protection of the old graveyard and Gledhill had been a decision of duty.

Her understanding after the incident with Lida had made him ashamed of the things he'd said to her. A lot of women would have made him pay for Lida, just on principle. He had certainly expected that very response. Yet instead of calling him to account, Perri had had enough faith in him to let it go. And a lot of women would have hammered on him forever because of what his mother, Leila, had done.

Yet Perri had stoically left Spirit, her only thought to defend her mother's reputation. For the first time, he'd allowed himself to wonder how she must have felt when she'd learned he was marrying Cadie.

She had stood up to him the day she'd acknowledged she was pregnant. Matt had trapped her against the door to the refrigerator and she had fearlessly held her ground.

As his gaze had roamed over to his wife, Matt had been forced to remember everything. *An honest woman.* A sobering thought. He, who had made such a fuss about "family," had declared they should divorce. And over what? He had cruelly told her flat-out that she couldn't fit into a family down here; into his world. Yet, how poisonous some of the women of "his world," of his family, had been for him.

His world had dictated that one woman was replaceable with another. Matt knew it just wasn't so. Losing Janie had left Sam a hollow man. And now the same thing had happened to him with Perri.

In the moonlight, Perri had looked exhausted, as if she'd cried herself to sleep. Matt had pictured her returning from Donnie's to a deserted house. Suddenly, that single act of disavowal had filled him with remorse.

Drawn by a deep-seated longing to the side of the bed, Matt had done his best to think it through. What was at the heart of his opposition to going to Tucson, he'd wondered? The hurt. To be open to knowing his grandfather was to be open to a well of grief. He would have to open up the very nucleus of his own wounded spirit.

Matt hadn't known if he could take that. In the past it had always been best not to put forth the effort. And then, he'd remembered the night of the lightning strikes. He had held himself apart from Perri that night as well, due to assumptions he had never questioned or explored. He hadn't known how to break through his pattern of stoic behavior then, either.

Perri had shifted in her sleep, curving herself into his hand. Until that moment, he hadn't been aware he was sitting beside her, gently stroking her bare hip. She'd smelled sweet, soft. His. *Don't run from me, honey,* he'd found himself praying. *Please.*

If he had been sober, he would have stayed. Cautiously so as not to wake her, Matt had released her and stood. He'd seized the gold locket Perri had left on the nightstand. It had gleamed in the moonlight spilling in through the window. Soundlessly moving out of Gledhill and through the night, Matt had crushed it so tightly in his hand, the chain had marked his palm.

Now, as the lonesome day gave way to evening, Matt tuned slowly back into his surroundings. He realized he'd pulled the necklace out of his pocket, seeking its comfort as if it were a talisman.

The horses sensed it first. Suddenly alert and back in the present, Matt halted as all around him equine uneasiness made it clear that something was about to happen. Flicking on the radio, he raced out to check the horizon in all directions.

Nothing. Yet. But he didn't like it. Vigilant in the certainty that something was coming, he thoughtfully pocketed Perri's locket. The weather bulletin was being broadcast as he moved back inside.

A heatburst. *And a woman alone in a storm.* He just knew Perri was at home, sitting right on top of a hill. "Holy God," he whispered in awe. Matt's body stilled somewhere deep inside as he grabbed for the phone. Unlike the swamp in his nightmare, incongruous and frozen solid, Spirit Valley was going to fry.

The ceiling fan above her went through the motions, but it was futile. Nothing stirred. It was the unimaginable heat that had finally brought her around from her nap. For almost four hours Perri had slept hard. Now she felt even worse. The heat, the man, and the damage to her marriage had her worn down.

As she dragged herself awake, Perri's despair enfolded her like a shroud. It had been only one day since Matt had made it plain she wasn't really a part of his family. *I feel like I've been run over,* she thought. How did people ever get anything done in the midst of despair? Everything in her acknowledged that this anguish was never going away.

She sat up, her movements slow and weary. Her throat hurt. It felt locked in unavailing sorrow. The muscles, as if protesting fate, were clenched and heavy. Perri brushed her hand over the place where her locket should have rested and almost wept. They hadn't even made it through the summer. They would never have a honeymoon.

Despair would always be present, she supposed, perhaps not

in an obvious way. Perhaps it would merely remain a low, dull undertone for long stretches of time. She might not be required to acknowledge it often, but losing Matt and her hope of family would be Perri's cornerstone of sorrow for the rest of her life. She was painfully conscious of her loss; brutally aware that she could do nothing to remedy the circumstances.

Sundown was just about upon her. Perri rested against the bumps and twists of the brass headboard and tried to breathe, willing herself into action.

For the second time in one day, she made it out of bed in a stupor. Perri vowed to fight her way through it, intent on another shower. She would let the water pound out the raw hurt and despair.

The answering machine caught her eye. There were seven new messages. "Now what?" Perri muttered. The impact of being out of touch as the sun rode so low in the sky finally registered. She turned the ringer back on and the phone immediately sounded to life.

"Where have you been?" he demanded before she could say hello. The static over the line gave Matt's voice a desperate edge.

No way was she awake enough for this. "I took a nap after the fridge was delivered," she replied with dignity. She was not going to mention that she had overslept. "And by the way," she reminded him in frosty tones, "you said you would have the old one moved—"

"Perri," Matt went on bullishly, "get in the basement. Now. There's a heatburst directly overhead. I have to see to the stock and my phone may not work for much longer."

"A heatburst? What does that mean?" she asked, not really caring.

"It means in about five minutes, there's gonna be nothin' between you and hell but barbed wire," he answered with deadly urgency. "And I don't have the time to give you a lesson in climatology. Get in the basement," he repeated. "I'll call when I can. And I'll come over as soon as possible. But I have to be here, maybe until it's over."

"I've never heard of a heatburst," she muttered. "Is it like a tornado?"

"Woman, if you are trying to drive me crazy, do it later. Now get your funny little butt down into that basement," Matt ground out the order. "And take the phone along in case they keep on working."

She could hear the sounds of wind and frenetic horses in the background. "Well, since you put it that—"

"Perri," he yelled as if trying to reach her over the wind, "don't make me have to worry for your safety. I'll come get you as soon as I can. Now git!"

"Okay, Matt," she replied loudly. "Be careful." There was a pause on the other end, as if he wanted to say more. She figured he just didn't trust her compliance.

Perri hung up and the phone rang immediately. In rapid succession she reassured first her mother and then Donnie. That done, she considered her next course of action. Whatever it was that was headed for the hill, those she loved were taking it seriously.

Throwing on some clothes, Perri listened to the television and received a quick course in weather as chaos. Suddenly wakeful and aware of the impending danger, she focused in on the report. Like a tornado, a heatburst was defined as supernatural wind. But a twister, selecting its victims at random, touched down, destroyed and moved on.

A heatburst, she learned, could go on for hours, causing dry, boiling clouds to hover over one area. *A hurricane without the water,* Perri realized. How delightful. She had never been through a heatburst. She had never mentally steeled herself for 80-to-100-mile-an-hour winds that might blow clear to dawn without abating.

The newscaster announced that an implosion of thunderstorms was causing a huge amount of root, tree and fence damage, and had already downed power lines in three counties. While Perri absorbed that bit of news, the woman went on to say that the collapsing storm had produced wind shears with enough force to bring down an airplane. She then turned matters over to the station's meteorologist for an update.

With the respectful tones of a church deacon, the weatherman took over. Solemnly, he informed his listeners that the air had become so electrically charged, the temperature had risen from ninety-one degrees to 112 in twenty minutes. Right over Spirit Valley.

"Terrific," Perri murmured.

The weatherman's tone was the one often used on Oklahoma television to describe the more lethal aspects of supernatural weather: A calm forbearance laced with an undertone of "Don't be an idiot. Head for the storm cellar."

"Very well," she vowed grimly. Perri grabbed a quilt and, moving quickly down the stairs, raced into the dining room. She took the time to cover the computer, lock up doors and windows, and grab her laptop. That done, she headed for the basement door off the back porch.

As she stepped onto the enclosed porch, the heat and the violence on the other side of the glass took her breath away. She watched as a wind roared onto the hill with the force of a stampede. Perri's first response was that the air was so hot, there was nothing to breathe. Her nose and ears closed up, and her throat felt sandy. Her involuntary gasping for air did nothing to relieve her speeding heart.

Oh my God, she thought with wonder. *It's like something out of the Old Testament.* The pressure of the boiling air was like nothing she had ever experienced. Matt's comment came back to her. There really *was* nothing separating her from hell but barbed wire. Perri tried to breathe, tried desperately to think straight. The air was so highly charged, her hair was standing on end.

She felt light-headed, nauseous and panicky. In addition to the usual places, she was instantly pouring sweat from her upper lip and between her shoulder blades. She noted that even the insides of her elbows were slick with pooling moisture. The weight of her T-shirt felt unbearable.

She braced against the refrigerator and willed herself not to faint. The deliverymen had moved the old fridge onto the back porch for her earlier in the day when they had installed the new one. It now stood near the basement door. Matt was supposed to have moved it down there so they would have a second refrigerator near the kitchen. But Matt hadn't been around.

Suddenly, the ceiling fan began to vibrate fit to come loose. A candy dish danced off the little table by the hot tub and landed on the braided rug. A loud, ripping noise out back just about stopped her heart. She watched in sorrow as a tree swiftly lost the battle and fell, upended at the roots. Then the tin roof on the old barn wailed as it began to lift away on one side.

She bolted for the basement door, hitting the light switches at the top of the stairs. Sweat burned her eyes, yet a sudden chill shivered up the back of her neck. Fear sent her stumbling halfway down the steps and into the basement, the laptop throwing her off balance in her haste.

As she turned back to pull the door shut, something slammed hard against it seconds after it latched. Perri then tried desperately to open it, just to see if she could.

It wouldn't budge. She was trapped. For now there was no way to go but down. So she took to the stairs.

For long moments, the coolness of the basement only made her feel more heated. But gradually, Perri calmed down. At least she was not going to faint. The familiar concrete smell soothed her and helped her get her breath back. Only then did she realize she'd forgotten the blasted phone. "So add that to my list of sins, Matt," she whispered.

The basement felt safe and protected from the cruel, heated world above. She looked around. Matt had been right; some of the furnishings stored down there were incredible. One part of her brain registered the fact that a portion of the basement could be made into some sort of family room when they needed it later on.

But then she remembered. They weren't going to need such a room. They weren't going to be a family. A wooden rocker by an old chest drew her eye and her heart. That, at least would work beautifully in the nursery. Frightened, lonely and exhausted, she sat down in the rocker. Perri tried not to think of how she might well be trapped until help arrived. She turned on a fan to get the air moving.

A ladybug crawled from the arm of the rocker onto the back of her wrist. Perri welcomed the company. As she crooned to her little companion, the two of them settled into a gentle rock.

Would Gledhill hold under this proud upheaval of nature? She wondered as she watched the ladybug journey into the valley between her knuckles. And what had hit the door like that?

Thinking straight when the world was turning upside down, was the key. She had nothing else to do at the moment but think. And she had nothing particularly pleasant to think about. The destruction of weather or the destruction of her marriage. Now there was a choice.

A low, angry rumble brought Perri back to her surroundings. "A hot, dry wind with enough force to roll a cloud," she recited. She waited patiently for the ladybug to crawl back onto the arm of the rocker before she stood up.

Perri didn't have to go out there to know how it felt. It only took once, being caught in a brutal wind to make a lifetime impression. One never forgot the whipping of dirt and grit; or the shock of ordinary objects turned into malevolent projectiles.

Perri rallied enough to find the stepladder and move it under one of the small basement windows. Shivering at the muffled sound of the savage storm, she perched on the ladder to watch wind and earth do battle. It was getting dark now, the backyard illuminated only by the yard lights.

Frozen in place on the stepladder, in a basement filled with cherished treasures of the past, Perri witnessed the upheaval of her ordinary world. Heat lightning fanned out in three directions to illuminate the night. It was something to see.

Fear of storms, discomfort in being confined to small places and the very real possibility she was trapped all melted away inside her. Being caught, unable to run, forced Perri into the wildness and the supernatural beauty of the storm.

Just then, metal screamed as the tin roof on the old barn finally broke loose and rolled itself up, like the lid on a can of sardines. Dazzled to witness heat, wind and lightning clash in the sky, all she could think of was Matt. He was out in that hell, protecting the present!

The tension was going to kill him. Matt yanked the sweat-stained bandanna from around his face and drew in a deep breath. It didn't help. It didn't do anything. The wind was rushing by so fast, it wouldn't stay put long enough for him to grab hold and breathe it in. His shoulders felt as tight as steel cables and just as weighty.

Sometimes it amazed him what he could accept and include just in the daily, ordinary act of living on the Plains. Tonight however, was truly out of the ordinary. Matt paused from taking a drink of water to witness lightning twist viciously through a roll cloud caught in the downdraft. It was impossible not to feel awe and wonder at the churning sky.

And the noise alone could drive a person mad. Yet, nothing had actually happened so far. In some ways that made the night more unbearable. Tension so permeated the air, there was no difference between his own tightly coiled soul and the hellish world around him.

Matt felt like kicking out a stall himself and breaking free. It was getting to the point where violence and destruction would have been a benediction. Some kind of a break, even a calamity, wouldn't get under his skin the way the lethal buildup of wind, dust and electrical charge was doing.

Fortunately, the Ransom place had been built so as not to provoke the temper of a storm. The original intention to crouch over the earth had been carried through from the old house to the stables and the outbuildings. By lying low, the Ransoms had time and again borne the lash of a whipping wind.

Of course, in bearing down into the earth the way they did, Matt reckoned the Ransoms often choked a little on the dust. But they never blew away. Gledhill, however, was poised on a hill and ready to take off.

"I should just go get her," he muttered desperately. The irony nesting in the fact that he had worked like the very devil to soothe and comfort some horses; and yet had offered his wife nothing but a scolding on the phone came home to him. Not knowing was weighing on him with each and every cry of the wind. He needed to know she was safe. He couldn't pry himself loose from thinking the worst any more than he could stop swearing at the phone when the answering machine kicked in every time he tried to call her.

Something had to break soon or he was going to go mad. It

had been too long a stretch of nerves, noise and heat. And where the devil was his father? Sam had been out-of-pocket since he had driven off in the car.

The night was too raw for clear thinking. Knowing he couldn't get through did nothing to subdue the pent-up urge to stab at the buttons on his cell phone. "Hell," he muttered as Gledhill's answering machine picked up yet again. That did it. Matt swore, killed the phone, and strode into the wind.

Eleven

She would want to be in that basement, he thought as he wiped his stinging eyes. Matt grimly approached the back door. "If not," he muttered, skirting a downed pecan tree, "she'd better be someplace out of harm's way. Somewhere ready with an explanation. Someplace," he decided, "like Arkansas."

Every bit of foliage had been ransacked. Breathing was futile. And when the wind didn't beat him down, the heat did. Yet Matt halted, awed by the sight of the rolled-up tin roof on the old barn. It was just this sort of thing he had feared.

A twister was one thing. It was lethal, relentless and mean. But a tornado moved on. Wind shears battering the hill for hours could wear down even the well-built courage of Gledhill.

He was grateful that Perri had left the backyard lights on so he could get the full effect. "At least it didn't fold," he reasoned, proud to see Gledhill holding fast. Proud and deeply relieved to see it with his own eyes. It somehow affirmed his hunch that Perri was all right.

Without warning, between one footfall and the next, and in the midst of chaos, it hit him. He loved Perri and he loved this place. And he had, all along. *What a time to finally figure that out,* he thought ruefully as he leaned into the wind.

Holding hard to the moment and to his own center, Matt understood how he had come to rely upon Perri to be the center for him. She had always made it conceivable for life to coil, uncoil, and spin around him. As he skirted the barn, he accepted the fact that he wasn't going to let her go. It just wasn't possible.

He had been a fool. No, he reasoned, he had been a fearful man. He gave thanks that she had thus far held the center for him. And if he had to call upon the parts of his heart that had been seared of all feeling, he would by damn do it. If he had to restore or repair that which had been injured, he would do that too. For Perri. Matt had never in his life been afraid of hard work.

He loved her and he'd just have to tell her and get her to stay with him. That was all. But first, he had to find her and then head on back to the horses. As he reached the back door, his heart stopped.

"Perri!" he cried. He was to the door of the basement before his mind or body registered the move. The blades of the fallen ceiling fan were wedged in between the basement door and the old refrigerator jutting out from the wall. He knew she was in there fighting to get out. She didn't quit in her attempt to break down the door at the sound of his voice. She kept on.

Matt paused, impressed by the fury with which she attacked the door. Gannie had always kept a claw hatchet mounted on the wall down there for just such an emergency. The way Perri was wielding it seemed personal.

Perri broke through the top half of the door and paused, breathing hard. With the sensitivity he usually reserved only for his horses, Matt remained silent and respectful in the closeness of her rage. He would have sworn he understood why she had paused. It was on her face.

Perri had broken through enough to feel free. She was panting and sweating and was determined. And finally she looked directly at him; including him in the moment. Without a word she carefully handed him the hatchet through the narrow opening, blade down and handle first.

Pulling the fan free with the claw, he quickly threw open what remained of the door. Observing her savage need to break out of the basement had shaken what was left of his restraint. "Why in the blazes didn't you take the damn phone?" Matt demanded, hauling her out. All the fear naturally funneled right into scolding her.

"I didn't take the damn phone because I forgot the damn phone," she responded angrily. "Put me down! You are not to snipe at me, do you understand?" Perri raged, thumping him for emphasis. "Just put me down."

"A pregnant woman should not be wielding a hatchet," he said decisively. Eyeing every possibility and subsequently rejecting each, the conclusion he was forced to draw didn't improve his mood. There was nowhere safe enough for Perri on the hill.

Matt eyed her cautiously as he gently set her on her feet. "Are you all right?" he asked, his hands moving over her to reassure himself.

"I'm fine, thank you," she replied with all the dignity she could muster. "The baby is fine."

"Good. Let's go," he said, taking her hand.

"Go where?" she asked, shocked at the idea of going anywhere. Perri pulled her hand away and glared at this madman.

"To Ransoms'," he answered.

She stared at him in disbelief. "You want to go out in that?" she squeaked. "Clouds, Matt, are being rolled upside down by the wind and you want to go out there?" She hitched a thumb in the direction of the old barn to add weight to the words.

"I want you with me," he said simply.

The reply stunned her. So did the understanding that on such a night she wasn't safe perched on the hill. The evidence lay at her feet.

"I want you with me," he repeated, herding her toward the door. "And I have to get back to the stock. I won't let anything happen to you."

They didn't get out fast enough to suit him. Matt was willing to wait while she sensibly traded flimsy sandals for cowboy boots and tucked her sleek little flashlight into one of them. But he was not about to wait while she traded her cutoffs for jeans. He planned to drive her straight to the door of Sam's place and march her right inside. A rather put-upon Mrs. Matt Ransom climbed into the pickup, regal as a queen.

Matt rounded the cab of the pickup to the driver's side and quickly got in. He started the engine and glanced at his wife. Matt didn't even bother to reproach himself for what he was thinking. He couldn't help but notice how hot she looked in cutoffs and cowboy boots and a light sheen of sweat.

Matt could only sigh and remind himself that he was no longer young and stupid enough to strip her down in a hundred-mile-an-hour wind. Besides, right now Perri looked so mad he was thankful she hadn't brought the hatchet. Feeling extremely noble, he shifted into drive.

In silent agreement, they headed around to the front for a quick look at the graveyard. It raised a unified sigh of relief to see that it would survive. Projectiles that once upon a time had been children's play equipment had tangled in the fence. The leg of a child's swing set was stuck in the graveyard gate.

"Condo litter," Matt grumbled, as he circled back around. But he was satisfied. The spare little arch had held; and the graves were as they had been for over a hundred years. They endured as a silent reminder of others who had witnessed winds tear apart the Plains.

The storm sounded even louder in the silence between them. For a man who had so recently determined that he really did love the woman by his side, Matt was remarkably hesitant to speak up. He glanced away from the pasture he was cutting through to look at her.

"You okay?" he asked, puzzled by her pensive expression.

"I'm fine, thanks," Perri answered politely. After a pause, she continued. "I've been thinking about what you said yesterday, of course. Thinking about reality. Reality, Matt, and the past," she said wearily. "I am so tired of butting heads with the past.

"I found some of Gannie's diaries stored in a trunk down in the basement. Did you know she fell in love with Ray Deepwater just before the war?" Perri asked.

"Ray Deepwater? No," Matt replied with surprise.

"I guess Ray must have been John's grandfather's brother. I'm a little hesitant to ask John, but I might just do it," Perri declared. "From what I can tell, her father didn't approve and Deepwater's father absolutely forbade their marriage. No wonder she refused to go back East to school," Perri mused. "No wonder she worked so hard to support herself."

"I've never heard any of this," Matt answered. "What happened?"

Perri fought back tears. "She waited out World War II for him. But he never made it back from the Pacific. And she never married. I think that is so sad. Gannie had waited for him to come home," Perri said somberly, "expecting to be disowned by her family when they married. She was fully prepared to help make a living when it happened," Perri murmured, once again lost in the past.

"I suppose that explains some things," Matt said, "like her special affection for John. It must have seemed peculiar at the time for Olivia Gledhill to set about learning how to support herself," he added, "instead of working toward making an 'appropriate marriage.' I always wondered why she never married."

Perri had found an entry in one of the diaries that had just about torn her heart. "I went out to the Fort Remount cemetery today," Gannie had written, "just for the quiet. Ray used to love to walk that hill. Now, to go through life without him, to never bear his children—to never build a life together—nor to ever be buried side by side, these things I must endure. I will never marry. But I will go there, often. To remember."

"No wonder she tried to guide my mother and me," she said unhappily.

"No wonder she became so focused on the past," Matt put in.

"Well, she made a best effort and lived with her choice," Perri said firmly. "So will I. I am sick to death of knuckling under to the past and being reasonable and polite." Perri looked away, disgusted with herself.

"You hurt me, Matt." She paused, as if weighing the consequences of words never spoken. "Why has that been so very hard to say?" she asked. "Why have I been protecting that one fact for so long? I wanted you to believe I was grateful I got out. I learned a lot and I've changed because of it. But I'm not grateful to you, Matt.

"I'm not grateful to you at all," she repeated with feeling. "I said that out of pride. I was being *nice* when I said that." Perri laughed sadly. "I've felt locked, frozen into being polite about how deeply you hurt me twelve years ago. I hate that! I was being nice about the fact that you broke my heart. I never wanted to leave Spirit," she whispered. "I wanted a family. Here."

"Perri, I didn't mean half of what I said yesterday," Matt replied softly. "You and I are not done, honey. But now is not the time for this." He was wary of her mood. No one should make snap decisions in a storm. It was best just to hang on and ride it out.

"We are done," she answered calmly. "I can't stay with a man who doesn't want me for myself. I can't stay and become the woman that would make me. And pretty soon, Matt," she declared, "you wouldn't be the man I was staying for."

"What?" he demanded.

"I won't end up locked in the past like Gannie and I won't run," she went on. "But I won't pine away either. I'm not going to spend my days living out the loss. You make a family where you are," Perri stated, "and where you are able. You've made it clear that I'm not a part of your family and I accept that," she said softly. "I'll just have to make one of my own."

Matt drove on, shocked into silence.

"I'll work with you for an amiable divorce, Ransom," she said. In spite of herself, she sounded reasonable, fair and polite. "I'll be staying right here. I'll make room for myself in Spirit if it's the last thing I ever do," she vowed. "I'll be doing what's best for the baby and for myself as a single mother."

She didn't see him wince at the term. "And I will do my part to make it easy for you to have a strong relationship with our child. But you're not getting custody," she continued forcefully when his eyes whipped around at her words. "So put that idea right out of your head."

Matt acknowledged silently that his remark about gaining custody had probably been his biggest mistake. "Perri, I don't want a divorce," he said firmly. "I want us to stay married." He was so sure that was all he had to say. Then everything would be fine between them.

"Matt, please," she said, as they drove toward the outbuildings. "I just don't have it in me to maintain the pretense of believing that. The only reason you wanted me in the first place was because I was forbidden. I was someone they said Matt Ransom couldn't have. Now all you want me for is the baby," she said in a matter-of-fact tone.

"Hold it!" he said, swerving to avoid a sheet of plywood loose in the wind. "Don't say that! I want the baby, of course. But I want you with or without the baby."

"Please don't insult my intelligence, Matt," she answered, grabbing hold of the gun rack as they struggled to clear the field. "You can't have it both ways. You've made it clear you will do anything, say anything, in order to accomplish what you have decreed must be done. And what 'must be done' in your estimation is to keep this baby here. You will say whatever you think I want to hear to get me to stay," she declared.

"But there's a flaw in your strategy, Ransom," Perri continued. "In order for it to work, I'd have to be stupid enough with love not to care that you really don't love me, or blind enough with love to believe that you do want me for me. Well," she reflected, "I'm neither." Perri looked away. "And I'm staying anyway, so you can drop the pretense.

"But you're right about one thing," she continued politely. "Now is not the time to discuss this. Maybe when I get back, we'll both have had time to think."

"Get back?" The look on Matt's face all but shouted his opposition.

"I plan to visit Tucson," Perri informed him. "I can take off after my amnio." She settled back into the silence as they drove on.

Matt stared straight ahead and slowly, carefully went through the motions of breathing. It wasn't just the atmospheric pressure that made it difficult. Alarm had locked his lungs up tighter than a wedge. At the moment, he had no resources to call upon to win her over. She was not going to give him another chance.

And why should she? He had never given her time to adjust. He'd just kept pushing. At the same time, he'd expected her to give him room while he took his own time to adapt to being married. To adjust to having her back; to loving her. Matt realized she didn't even know that he was in love with her. He hadn't shared it with her.

Although he was practically sweating bullets, he no longer felt the heat building around him. He felt frozen, locked inside his point of view. A prisoner of his own strategy. In his nightmare, it had been the frozen countryside Matt had battled through to reach her. In reality, the red earth around him baked in the night. It was his iced-over emotions that were guilty of driving her away. He had been unwilling to give her what he had demanded for himself.

All along his ace had been that she loved him. He had taken it for granted that Perri would remain the center for him. And in pushing her to accommodate his needs, he'd pushed her right out of his life.

He drove on. Gledhill hadn't crumbled. Ransom's held. The one thing that had been blown apart was the one thing he had felt in his heart would always remain constant. That Perri would love him long enough for him to find his way back to loving her.

"What do I have to do to get you to stay with me?" Matt demanded hoarsely. "What do I have to say?"

A muffled crash from the other side of his father's house saved him from making things worse. They both held their breath as the sound of a car horn carried over from the entrance to the property. It was beating out an SOS. *Sam*, he thought desperately. "Get out," he ordered, pulling up and braking hard by his front porch.

"No," she replied grimly. "You may need me. Don't waste time!"

He didn't. The pickup headed toward the horn. As they reached the front, Matt swore viciously at the sight between them and the highway.

The wrought-iron arch at the entrance had been brought down.

It looked as if the side, or probably the roof of an eighteen-wheeler had been turned into a sail. Siding, tumbled by the storm, had clipped the top of the arch, sending it to the ground. The road onto the property was blocked by fallen trees, mangled aluminum and ironwork. His father's car had been chased into the windbreaks.

"He must have figured that he couldn't make it on the straight-away and headed into the trees," Matt said tightly as they drove hard to reach the damaged car. He threw the pickup into park and flew out the door. It barely registered when Perri scooted into the driver's seat and completed a turnaround.

Matt cursed the wind. Sam's beloved trees were damaged, obscuring Matt's view of the driver's side. His eyes burning, unable to see, he fought hurriedly through broken branches. But he just couldn't find a way to get to the car.

He couldn't get to his father. Matt coughed at the sandy feeling of tainted wind rushing into his lungs. Grief, despair and anger shot through him. The car was almost buried in the broken trees and debris.

A closer look, however, revealed that it wasn't that bad. Matt gave thanks, relieved to note that the arch had only smashed the car's trunk and the back portion of the roof. Mercifully, Sam had avoided ramming into a tree. One headlight still worked.

"Is he all right?" Perri demanded, aiming her flashlight toward the driver's side. She could barely see with the dirt blowing. The familiar, dreaded pain of heat and grit and wind ravaging the eyes hit her immediately.

She battled to steady the beam and stay upright. For the first time Perri got the full rage of the wind. The force was so strong, it kept driving her forward into the angry tangle of broken branches and siding. Dizzy with the heat blasting into her, she licked her lips and tasted the grit.

Thin wires of heat lightning streaked out of the south as the car's overhead light came on and Sam carefully squeezed through the door on the passenger's side. They watched, anxious and helpless to assist, as he slowly battled his way through the barbed-wire fence and into the west pasture. Sam signaled forward at their shouts and headed briskly along the fence until he was in the clear. Matt grabbed Perri, and in relief they tracked him from their side of the wire.

Illuminated by the one working headlight and Perri's flashlight, Matt held the wire as Sam carefully worked his way through. The wind seemed to slow down around him, as if adjusting to a force equal to its own. Sam Ransom stood unbending and grimly eyed his damaged trees, his damaged car, his fallen iron arch and his obstructed road.

"Sam, talk to me!" Perri demanded, studying him under the beam of her flashlight. "How are you?"

"Annoyed," Sam said, leading them back for a closer look at the damage. "Annoyed about covers it, honey. We're going to have to call the tree surgeon and get on his list." Sam politely turned her hand so the flashlight shone into Matt's sweating eyes instead of his own.

"He could care less that his car is wrecked, sweetheart," Matt replied dryly. He blinked at the light and the grit in his eyes. "He's just mad about his trees and a little peeved that he couldn't outrun that arch." Matt was more shaken than his father. It was obvious. He started hollering.

"You had to try and outrun it, didn't you?" he demanded, ignoring the fact that he would have done the same thing. "You just had to prove you could. What if that thing had fallen faster? I have enough to worry about without having to cut you out of a car wreck." There, he'd said it. "And do you mind telling me where the hell you've been?"

"I almost made it!" Sam countered. He ignored his shouting son and smiled at Perri. "I'd already committed myself to the turn when that arch started to go. There was nothing else to do but outrun that devil. And no," he said, looking at Matt, then Perri. "I'm not going to the emergency room."

Matt looked insulted. "Did I suggest such a thing?" he demanded. "Dad, why didn't you call?"

The grit felt like all of the desert had lodged between her teeth. She hated the sound of it in her mouth. Perri flinched, her head jerking to the side when a slender branch turned vicious and slapped her hard across the jaw. The blow knocked her against a chunk of mangled siding. She cried out suddenly and was on her way down.

She had no chance to avoid the raw, jagged edge of a broken limb as it rolled under her feet. It happened fast. There was no time to recover before she was dragged down by the wind, caught in a lethal undercurrent.

Matt's quick grab kept her from being impaled through the throat on an unyielding spike of broken limb. He pulled her up and back, carrying her away from the lethal mass that seemed almost alive with vengeance.

Then Matt wouldn't let her go. If he could have pulled her inside him, it wouldn't have been enough. He'd never had a chance to tell her he loved her.

Sam faced his son in a fury that rivaled the night. "What is she doing out in this?" he demanded. "Perri's not dressed to be out here without losing half the skin off her legs just by standing still. You yourself wouldn't come out dressed in shorts." He pointedly eyed the bandanna tied around Matt's neck.

"Come on back to the house with me," Perri said, taking Sam's arm, and the opportunity. She ignored her trembling. Matt tried to hold her even closer. "Since you won't go to the hospital—"

"Honey, I'm fine," Sam interrupted with a gesture that let her know to stay out of it. He turned to straighten out his son. "I'll start clearing away what I can," Sam declared in a low, dangerous tone. "See to your wife and make sure she calls her mother. I assured Janie you would take care of Perri. Now don't make me a liar."

"So that's where you've been," Matt said with sudden understanding, noting how sharp his father looked for a man who'd just crawled through a fence. Matt gently relaxed his hold on Perri and shook out his aching hand. He'd bent his thumb backward when he'd made the grab. Only now did the pain hasten through him.

He put physical pain and aching emotions aside as he knew he must. He dared not think about how he had almost lost her. The fear that had twisted through him since he'd heard Sam's SOS, Matt buried deep. Now was not the time to start sweating over what might have happened. There was work to be done; and deep emotions would just get in the way.

His dad was his old self. Perri was safe, sheltered in his arms from the wind. He had gotten to her in time. He would be content with that. Matt's relief was faintly tinged with despair. He would let himself feel when he could. If he could.

Taking the flashlight from Perri, Sam started barking orders. "Get her to the house. Then check on the stock and come back here. Pronto. And Matt," Sam whispered to his son's back as Matt escorted his wife to the pickup, "don't mess it up this time."

By sunrise, the storm was played out.

Twelve

Matt must have watered, Perri thought. Obviously someone had cleared away the storm debris while she had slept. They hadn't seen each other since Matt had driven her back to Gledhill sometime around dawn. He had ordered her to bed and headed back. Perri had barely had the opportunity to thank him for saving her life.

She'd headed straight for the shower. As she had breathed deeply, letting the shower's warmth and moisture cleanse her lungs, Perri had started to shake. It had finally hit her how easily one of them could have been killed or seriously injured. She had welcomed the water stinging into the cuts on her legs. The sharp pain had alerted her to the fact that she was alive.

Perri had given thanks her family had made it through almost unscathed before falling into bed. What sleep she had gotten had been fretful. And she doubted Matt or Sam had been to bed yet.

Now, she let the steamy scent of water on warm concrete ground her in the present like nothing else could. Remarkably, there was no evening wind. The sweet, damp smell of the honeysuckle, what was left of it, played around her. Water always intensified its lush quality. She looked forward to the time for rain.

She moved to the door and studied the dirt floor of the old barn in the light of evening. The earth seemed energized by its recent exposure to the sky. It glowed a dusty pink, shades lighter than the surrounding soil.

Perri looked up. The light coming in the barn from the open roof changed everything about the structure. She stepped inside, drawn by the peaceful way the evening shadows altered the familiar old building.

The acoustics had been modified dramatically by the rolled-up roof. Locusts in the surrounding trees emptied their anxious hum into the sound-sensitive space. The wind remained still. Spent. Not even the tin roof clattered.

Perri smoothed her palms lovingly over her belly and looked west. Broad, soft ribbons of copper and aqua were showcased in the barn's open doorway. And Matt stood in the shadows. Abruptly, the locusts paused, the silence going deep. It was thorough, startling and complete. And in the silence, as she watched the fireflies wink around them, Matt crossed the threshold into the barn and came toward her.

Perri silently viewed his approach. She could only wait for him to reach her. Grief slowed a person down. Whenever grief was in command it took every bit of remaining life just to move through the everyday, mundane rituals of existence.

Matt continued toward her, steady, confident and strong. His footsteps struck the earth, sounding so right. Matt belonged here.

Her desperate need to weep remained tightly reined. It lodged in her throat, an ache for which there would be no immediate relief. She hadn't run. He'd come back. They'd survived the storm and the night. Apart.

"Thank you for clearing away the wreckage and dealing with the back porch," she said. "I'm grateful to you." Trying for calm, Perri took a deep breath. "So, who did you call first, Matt," she asked, "the roofer or the tree surgeon?"

"The travel agent," Matt replied quietly. "And your grandmother Anne, in Tucson." After a moment, he smiled faintly. "She sounds wonderful, hon. Five minutes on the phone with her and I felt like I'd known her all my life. I, uh, spoke to my grandfather,'' he said, his voice gruff.

"I'm glad for you, Matt," Perri replied.

"He says he wants a chance to get to know me. Somehow, I found myself agreeing that they should come here to visit us." He seemed a little bewildered as to exactly how that had happened. Perri knew her grandmother. She could just imagine.

"Anne insisted they could house-sit while we go to San Francisco," he said. "Your grandmother sounded like she had the whole thing already planned. She seemed to relish the idea of supervising the renovations. So, do you still want to go to San Francisco," he asked. "Shall I tell them to come on?

"Or we could visit them, if you prefer," he added when she didn't respond. "There's a racetrack in Tucson, Rillito Park— the oldest one in the Southwest. I'd like to take you to see it. We could book one of those cottages at the Arizona Inn," Matt said cautiously, "drive out to watch the sunset at Gates Pass."

Perri blinked, stunned by his words. If he meant it, could she handle it? The question disturbed her. She'd never prepared herself for any dramatic shift in Matt. She'd never thought such a thing possible. She had always expected she would have to work around him.

Did she have the courage to trust that he could change; that he would change for her? She wondered. Perri stared at the sunset, letting doubt wash over her. If Matt could make an alteration, then she would have to alter yet again to accommodate it.

He watched worry darken her eyes, making the shards of amber most prominent. "You're not going to give me another chance, are you?" Matt asked quietly. "I can see it in your eyes. You don't believe I can change."

"Most people can't, Matt," Perri cautioned, "even if they want to desperately."

"You did," Matt reminded her.

"I had to," she answered forcefully. Change was certainly a skill that the events of her life had honed fine. "I didn't have any other choice. I lost it all. You're losing nothing," she reminded him. "Change is painful, slow and lonely. Nobody changes unless they have to, in my opinion." Perri broke away.

She couldn't bear to stand so close to him. She loved him and the ache in her throat was the desperate longing for a family.

"Change leaves you shaky, Matt," she went on more quietly. The effort to explain took her back into the hurt. "It uses all your courage. And no matter how hard you work at it, no matter how far you go," she reflected, "you're never that far removed from what you were.

"Even 180 degrees isn't far enough," she said, turning away from him as if to protect, to keep private that last shred of truth. "You wake up one morning certain in the knowledge that you're just the opposite side of the same familiar coin. And that coin is in the currency of longing and regret. Of yearning, Matt," she said. "Yearning for what you've lost, for what you lost the chance to have. There's always a silent longing for what you had to change from."

Matt didn't respond. He stood there and let her get it out. For once he didn't push; didn't try to impel her to bend.

"You've never had to change, Matt," she said. "Believe me, you can't holler it done. It's easier to simply announce that you can't do it and have everybody work around you. Make everyone else adjust.

"And why would you change when you don't have to?" she asked, turning toward him. "I'm not taking our baby away from here, away from family. However shaky or disjointed it may be, this is where my baby's family lives." She stood before him for one final question. "What would you change for?"

"For you," he said quietly, closing the remaining space between them. The last of the light glinted off the locket he held in his palm. Warm fingers closed over hers as he put it into her hand.

Perri searched his eyes for the truth and found it in the dwindling light of sundown. She knew him. She knew that if Matt said he would do it, he would. Perri saw all the courage and skill he possessed focused on their future. She smiled. "You mean it. Don't you?" she asked softly.

Matt stood unflinching in the presence of her hesitation. Perri deserved the truth. It was more than he could take to think of losing her. "Yes, I do," he whispered as his eyes filled. "I love you, Perri. You *are* a part of my world. The best part. *You're* my family," he declared. "If Gannie was the backbone, honey, you are the heart."

Matt opened his arms and she joyfully rushed to him. He held her fiercely enough to take her to the edge of pain. She didn't mind.

"I don't expect I'll be any good at it at first," he said pulling back to look at her. "But I love you so much, and I can bend. I can't live without you, hon."

If things get better; if you get what you want; Perri believed you damn straight better have enough courage to meet it. Breathless from his kiss, she smiled. "So, honey, how was your day?" she inquired.

Matt laughed out loud and hugged her with obvious delight. Night was approaching; the air had transformed. He could feel it. Gledhill and Spirit Valley were at peace.

She stood gazing at him in the darkening preserve of light, delighting in the way the laughter lit up his eyes. Holding the locket of promise close to her heart, Perri knew they would finally be a family—forever.

*   *   *   *   *

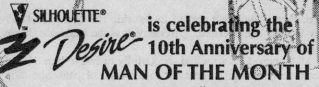

SILHOUETTE® _Desire®_ is celebrating the 10th Anniversary of MAN OF THE MONTH

For ten years Silhouette Desire has been giving readers the ultimate in sexy, irresistible heroes.

So come celebrate with your absolute favorite authors!

MAN of the Month

JANUARY 1999
BELOVED by Diana Palmer—
SD #1189 Long, Tall Texans

FEBRUARY 1999
**A KNIGHT IN RUSTY ARMOR
by Dixie Browning—**
SD #1195 The Lawless Heirs

MARCH 1999
**THE BEST HUSBAND IN TEXAS
by Lass Small—**
SD #1201

APRIL 1999
BLAYLOCK'S BRIDE by Cait London—
SD #1207 The Blaylocks

MAY 1999
LOVE ME TRUE by Ann Major—
SD #1213

Available at your favorite retail outlet, only from

Silhouette®

SILHOUETTE®

Desire®

is proud to present
a sensual, exotic new miniseries from
Alexandra Sellers
*Powerful sheikhs born to rule and destined
to find love as eternal as the sands...*

SONS
OF THE
DESERT

SHEIKH'S RANSOM (SD #1210, April '99)
His country's heirloom jewel had been stolen, and
Prince Karim vowed to recover it—by kidnapping the
thief's fiancée, socialite Caroline Langley. But this
sheikh-in-disguise didn't expect the primitive stirrings
that she aroused.

THE SOLITARY SHEIKH (SD #1217, May '99)
Prince Omar's heart was as barren as the desert—until
beguiling Jana Stewart, his daughters' tutor, tempted the
widower's weary soul like an oasis.

BELOVED SHEIKH (SD #1221, June '99)
Prince Rafi could have a harem of women...but he desired
only one: Zara Blake. Then the bewitching woman was
abducted by his arch enemy! Would the beloved sheikh
rescue fiery Zara to make her his mistress...or his queen?

Available at your favorite retail outlet.

Silhouette®

SILHOUETTE® Desire®

COMING NEXT MONTH